After the Storm

The Story of

Hannah Applegate Benson Stone

Book I of Hannah's Legacy

By Cary Flanagan

Also, By Cary Flanagan:

"Moon Dance – A Quilter's Creative Journey"

Twelve Innovative Quilt Designs

Published and distributed by Nancy Dill,
QuiltWoman.com,

info@quiltwoman.com Copyright 2009"

"Sarah's Quest: A Place to Belong."

Book II in the "Hannah's Legacy" Trilogy

Copyright © Cary Flanagan, 2021

"You will find yourself easily engaged in the lives of Hannah and her extended family, their trials and triumphs in After the Storm. Cary Flanagan weaves a lovely story of a young woman — a quilter — and her life in rural 19th century New Hampshire. I particularly enjoyed the way the author told the story both from the viewpoint of Hannah as a young girl through her diary writings and from her recollections as an adult looking back on her life. As a quilter, you will enjoy how quilting forms the backdrop for the story. As both a quilter and non-quilter, you will be inspired by Hannah's resilience."

Morna McEver,

Founder/CEO International Association of Creative Arts Professionals, and Creative Arts Business Summit.

www.joinICAP.com

"An intimate and authentic glimpse into life in rural 19th century New England. This tender portrayal of love, loss, and resilience and the potential healing power of family, friends, and community, invite you to ponder the gifts and challenges of your own ancestry."

Edie Hartshorne,

MSW, musician, artist, and author of Light in Blue Shadows.

"After the Storm" is a riveting novel written by Cary Flanagan. More than anything else, the book reminds us of the fragility of the human condition and one's ability to overcome obstacles and setbacks. This book ended all too quickly for me as I really enjoyed it. Yet, the characters were fully developed, and the ending was satisfying. I would highly recommend this as a "good read."

Patricia,

Amazon reader.

Publisher:

Cary Flanagan

ISBN: 978-1-7374754-1-5

I dedicate this book to my mother,

Elsa Fay Hartshorne Craig

from whom I inherited my love of all things creative and beautiful.

And my grandmother,

Sarah Eliza Proctor Fay

Who sewed most of the clothing for her family on a treadle sewing machine.

Acknowledgements:

Many people helped me in developing my story, researching nineteenth century New Hampshire village life, reading early drafts, editing my text, and creating beautiful artwork. To each of the following people, I owe a debt of gratitude!

First, a heartfelt Thank You to Linda Drew Smith, Vice President of the Madison, New Hampshire Historical Society, for an interesting and informative oral history of the town, its buildings, and inhabitants, going back several generations. I am much obliged to her also for providing me with several books and pamphlets related to the history of Madison, and a detailed map of the town dating to 1892. Thanks also to the staff members of the Historical Society who showed me several early maps from the 1860s and provided additional information.

For reading early drafts of my novel and offering feedback, encouragement, and constructive criticism, I thank Cathy Bowen, Gemma Geisman, Robin Hartshorne, Marianna Hartsong, Beth Helfter, Laurel Matsuda, and Terri Sontra. I deeply appreciate your contributions to this book.

For professional editing, constructive criticism, and guidance I thank Sonja Hakala of Full Circle Press LLC.

For coaching and supporting me in the final stages

of preparing my manuscript for publication and for offering valuable advice regarding marketing options, I offer special thanks to Edie Hartshorne, for her insights, encouragement, and for sharing her own experiences in publishing.

For outstanding cover design and artwork, I thank Artist Ashley Santoro (Reedsy). I look forward to future collaborations.

Most of all my deepest thanks and appreciation go to my husband Ron, for believing I could do this and for putting up with me for many months while I have been busy gestating and birthing this book. I love you.

"I am not afraid of storms for I am learning how to sail my ship."
Louisa May Alcott

Prologue: July 5, 2005

Immersed in her work Becca moved the fabric back and forth in a steady rhythm under the needle. This was her favorite kind of day—no appointments, no commitments, no interruptions. She had even taken the phone off the hook. Soft instrumental music played in the background. She had a whole day to work on her latest art quilt. What bliss!

The quilt was nearly finished, and now Becca was laying down the final layers of silky stitches in many shades of gold and orange, pink, purple and green to bring out the subtle shadings of the image, painting with thread. She loved the feel of the fabric under her fingers and the color shifts she was creating made her feel giddy with pleasure.

She was so absorbed in her work that when the doorbell jangled, she jumped, and several stitches went skittering off sideways. "Shoot!" she said. "Now I will have to pick out all those stitches!"

When the doorbell rang a second time, Becca peeked around the curtain in her studio window to see who had come to interrupt her day. There was a UPS truck parked right outside the front door of her townhouse. "I haven't ordered anything," she thought, a bit annoyed but also curious.

Resigned, she went downstairs to open the door. The driver, wearing the traditional UPS brown shorts and a short-sleeved shirt to suit the summer weather, reached a clipboard over an enormous box. "Sign here," he said, pointing and she did. "This box is very heavy. I will help you get it inside but that is as far as I can go. Sorry."

"I can manage," Becca said. However, when she took hold of her side of the box she nearly dropped it. "Wow! What the heck is in this thing anyway?"

"Dunno," the driver said, pushing the enormous package just inside the front door. "I just deliver 'em." He shrugged and turned to go. "I hope you have someone who can help you with that," he called as he climbed into his truck.

Becca stared at the box her quilting forgotten. There were large labels on each side of it marked "FRAGILE!" and "THIS SIDE UP!" She went into the kitchen to her "magic" drawer—the one which held everything she might need for any given situation. After rummaging for a moment, she found the box cutter and returned to the front hall with mounting excitement.

It did not take long to cut away the top and sides of the box then pull off layers of packing material. Becca gasped in astonishment. There stood a beautiful antique treadle sewing machine that someone had clearly loved and cared for. The wood of the cabinet and drawers glowed with many years of handling and polish. The cast iron legs gleamed black, showing off the intricate designs of interwoven vines.

Carefully wedged below the cabinet and obscuring the treadle was a clear plastic bag through which Becca glimpsed a variety of colors. She pulled the bundle gingerly from its resting place and opened the top of the bag. Inside she found a large manila envelope with her name on it and under that, protected by layers of tissue paper, was a quilt unlike any she had seen before.

Becca tore open the seal on the envelope, hoping to find an explanation for the arrival of these treasures. Inside she saw a handwritten letter and a faded typewritten manuscript. There was also a yellowed envelope containing several quilt patterns, written on fragile paper and showing wear from much use. She withdrew them with great care and saw that they included diagrams as well as written instructions. Dates at the top of each pattern, written in a fine hand, ranged from 1890 to 1915.

On the back page of the letter, she found her Grandmother Rachel's signature.

"Dearest Becca," the letter began. *"I am pleased to pass on to you this family heirloom. This was your Great Great Grandma Hannah's sewing machine, given to her by her first husband, Aaron Benson, early in their marriage, most likely about 1879. She treasured this machine above all her personal possessions. Only her love and devotion to her family and her God came before her love of sewing, and only one other person in the entire county in which she lived had*

a similar machine at that time. That was her Aunt Rebecca, who raised Hannah and for whom you were named.

The letter continued. *"You will find a manuscript that Hannah dictated to me not long before she died, and which I typed up at her request so that future generations of the family might come to know what it was like to grow up in rural New England in the 19th century. Unfortunately, she was unable to complete her dictation due to her failing health so I have included an account of the remainder of her story as best I can.*

"Granny Hannah also kept a journal throughout most of her life and I have included portions of it in this manuscript. The original belongs to your Aunt Julia if you are interested in seeing it.

"Granny Hannah was a fine seamstress, quilt maker, and quilt designer. She had a very inquisitive and creative mind and was very much ahead of her time in establishing a successful quilt pattern business as well as being a loving wife, mother, and grandmother. I have included several of her patterns and one of her most treasured quilts in this package. This is your legacy, Becca. I have seen many traits in Granny Hannah that have flowed down through the generations and now they are reflected in you."

Becca stopped reading the letter for a moment, touched by her grandmother's words. Then her curiosity about the quilt overcame her desire to read more. She carefully unwrapped and unfolded the quilt then laid it out on the sofa in her living room. The clarity of the colors and the movement and energy within each block stunned her. The quilt was in almost pristine condition. Only a few signs of age and wear were visible, a true rarity in a quilt that was more than

120 years old.

A noted quilt historian and collector had come to speak to Becca's quilt guild the previous year and had told the members that sometimes quilt makers in the 19th century made a quilt that was out of the ordinary for its time. Often, makers of such quilts put them away for safekeeping rather than share them with others or actively use them at home. The quilt in Becca's hands came down through four generations of her family and each recipient had honored Hannah's request to preserve it. That certainly explained why the colors were still so vivid!

Becca recognized a block design similar to the traditional "North Wind" block used in the quilt but the quilt itself was different from any she had seen before. It was made of scrap fabrics using colors that encompassed almost the full spectrum of the color wheel. They were bright and "happy" colors. There were also changing values, light fabrics, as well as dark, which made it seem as if a strong wind were indeed blowing across the surface of the quilt. It made her feel joyful, just to look at it.

Becca could see the intricate lines of the beautiful hand stitched quilting but when she looked at how the pieces were joined together, it was obvious the quilt had been pieced by machine. On the back was a label that read, in neatly embroidered letters, "After the Storm, made by Hannah Benson, October 1885." It took Becca's breath away to think that Granny Hannah pieced this quilt on this very treadle machine, and now it was hers!

Her hands shaking, Becca continued reading the

letter.

"*Granny Hannah came to live with our family in Conway, NH in 1949, a few years after her beloved Ben died of a massive heart attack. She had continued to live on in the house that he had built for her and their family on the main street of the village until she was over ninety, making quilts and quilt patterns as long as she was able. Her eldest son, Jacob, and most of her other children settled in the area and raised their families there. Only her daughter Sarah was absent, having left home for the Arizona Territories when she was seventeen, one of the great sorrows of Granny Hannah's life.*

"*Your grandfather George and I were finally able to prevail upon her to leave her enormous house and move in with us as her eyesight worsened and she became less steady on her feet. She was no longer as straight and tall as she had been and her once clear blue eyes had dimmed greatly so that she could no longer read or, most painful of all, sew. She tired easily and napped often. However, her snowy hair was still thick and long and her mind was still razor sharp for someone her age, and she was just as feisty and independent as she had been all her life.*

She insisted on having her own space in the house and bringing her beloved treadle sewing machine with her, the very one you see now. She had apparently made up her mind that I should have it after she was gone since I was the only quilt maker among her grandchildren. I was thrilled that she chose me, I can tell you! I did not find the journals until after she passed on when I was going through her things. She kept them secret until then. I have read most of the entries. They are fascinating, though, of course, I already knew most of her story by then.

"My two older children loved Granny Hannah and enjoyed spending time with her, listening with rapt attention to the stories she told about when she was their age growing up in a small village near the White Mountains. Your mother was born the same year Granny Hannah came to live with us, so she never got a chance to know her remarkable namesake. However, baby Hannah kept us company in her cradle during those long sessions when Granny and I recorded her life story, the same cradle that rocked her as an infant as well as her own children and grandchildren.

"I was heartbroken when Granny left us. She took a bad fall on the flagstones in our downstairs hallway when no one was home. I later found her sitting in her favorite chair in the living room with blood on her face and clothing and one very black eye where her glasses had cut into the skin. It was scary to find she had no memory of falling and when we took her to the hospital, the doctor told us she most likely had had a small stroke and then suffered a concussion in the fall. She was never 'quite right' after that, and so we were unable to finish recording her story.

"It was your Aunt Julia's 'job' to wake Granny every morning and bring her tea. Not long after Granny's fall, Julia came to me in the kitchen crying, "Mommy—I can't get Granny Hannah to wake up!" I went to her room and found Granny lying peacefully in her bed with a happy smile on her lips. It was a comfort to me to know that she had died quietly in her sleep, perhaps dreaming of her lost loves, Aaron, and Ben. I missed her greatly after she was gone, but I like to think that she reunited in heaven with both her cherished husbands, her beloved mother, and Aunt Rebecca and with all the kin and friends who had gone before her.

"So now, my dear granddaughter, you are in possession of a long treasured antique Singer treadle sewing machine,

17

as well as a highly prized quilt and some of your great great grandmother's original quilt designs and patterns, along with a faithful transcription of her own words. Take good care of them! I am hoping that with your creative mind and technical abilities, you will find some use for them. Perhaps you can find a way to turn these treasures into a book so you can share Granny Hannah's remarkable memoir with a wider audience.

"One thing I want to note about the manuscript: There were many times during our recording sessions when Granny would comment on something directly to me or I might prompt her to remember something in particular. I have decided to delete those asides in the interest of clarity, so that what you have here is a straight narrative in Granny Hannah's own words.

"Be sure to keep in touch and let me know when your next art quilt exhibit will be. I love the work you are creating now, and I cannot wait to see how your designs and techniques evolve from here. Perhaps Granny Hannah has found a way to live on in you!

"All my love, dear Becca, Your grandmother, Rachel"

Becca sat, stunned, for several minutes, holding the letter in shaking hands, and letting her grandmother's words sink in. "I wonder what I can do with these treasures," she said to herself.

Then she settled into her favorite reclining chair in the living room with the beautiful antique quilt spread out in front of her on the couch and began to read the tissue-thin pages of the manuscript.1

Chapter One

Transcript of a memoir dictated in 1950 by Hannah Stone to her granddaughter Rachel Bradley when Hannah was ninety-two years old.

I have been on this earth a very long time, and before I meet my Maker, I want to share something about my life, the people, and the experiences that have been so important in guiding and shaping the woman I am now. I also want to share what it was like to grow up in "the olden days."

Life can be very cruel sometimes. I have learned some difficult lessons over the years and have suffered many sorrows, but I have many happy memories as well, and they help to make up for the hard times.

I was raised by a remarkable and gifted aunt, I have loved and been loved by two good men, and I have borne six children who have graced and filled my world in ways that are difficult to express. Many grandchildren and great-grandchildren, surround me, all of whom bring me joy and comfort. I have been luckier than most women of my time to have been able to spend my days and years doing those things I have always loved best: raising my family, sewing, and creating beautiful quilts, cultivating my gardens, giving love and assistance where I could, and living my faith. I have truly lived a good life, and I am grateful.

I was born August 27, 1858, just a few years before the terrible war between the North and the South, though of course I did not know anything about that until much later. I was born in an old farmhouse near a small village some distance south of Mt. Washington, the largest and most imposing of the so-called White Hills of New Hampshire.

My parents' farm was small—just a few acres of rocky ground on the side of a hill, not much compared to some. There were few families in the village itself at that time. Our little town did not begin to grow and prosper until after the railroad came, built right through the center of it some years later. It was the kind of place where everyone looked out for each other, including those, like my parents, who lived on hardscrabble farms in the surrounding hills.

That farm is long gone. The buildings burned some years after my parents died, and all there is to see now are stone-lined cellar holes where the house and barn once stood. I went back to see it when I was much older. There were towering trees growing in the rooms where we once lived, and brambles covered the foundation. At least the scrubby apple trees in the small orchard had somehow survived, as well as the old stone walls surrounding what had once been open pasture. Now there is only forest and silence.

My earliest real memory is of my mother crying

inconsolably. I was perhaps three. Other people had come to the house, but no one would tell me why she was crying until finally my Aunt Rebecca gently set me on her lap and told me that Mama was sad. I vaguely remembered when my father went away with many other men from the village, and my mother held me up and waved my arm to the men marching by. My mother was sad then too, but this was different. My aunt tried to explain that my father had gone far away to fight in a war and would never be able to come home. I wanted to know why, but she just cried then too.

Not long after that, my mother became seriously ill. The curtains in her bedroom covered the small windows, and the room was dark and smelled funny. Aunt Rebecca stayed in the house to take care of her and me. I would slip into Mama's room and lie beside her, but she was asleep most of the time. I do not think she even knew I was there.

Early one morning a crash of thunder woke me suddenly. I was snuggled against Mama's back, and when I grabbed her for comfort, she was very still, and her skin was cold. She did not look like my mama anymore and did not answer when I called her name. I screamed. Aunt Rebecca came and held me tight. I can still remember the sound of pouring rain on the rooftop and outside the window of Mama's bedroom, and the wind and thunder. I was so scared.

"What has happened to Mama? Why can't she hear me?" I sobbed.

"She has gone to a better place, to be with your father in heaven," Aunt Rebecca said, tears running down her checks.

"Did I do something bad?" "Why has she left me?" "Why can't I go with her?" "When will she come back?" Neither my aunt nor the people who came to visit our house knew how to answer such difficult questions from a small child. They were kind and said "poor child" to me, but I did not understand why.

Then the terror came: "Who will take care of me," I wailed.

"I will," my aunt told me, wrapping me in her arms.

Aunt Rebecca took me to live with her in a house in the village that she had inherited from her parents. At first, I did not want to go, in case my mother came back and could not find me. I tried to hold onto my mother's bedpost, then a table leg, then the railing of the porch, begging my aunt to let me stay. All that time the rain was pouring down, and once we left the shelter of the porch, we were soon soaked to the skin. My aunt wrapped me in her shawl and carried me out to the wagon. She said everything would be all right. Unwillingly, I went with her, my face dripping with rain and tears. All I brought with me was my nightdress, a day dress, and a simple cloth doll my mother had made for me before she took sick. I resolved in my heart then that one day, Mama would come and find me, and we would never be apart again.

My aunt lived in a fine house, painted white with dark green shutters on either side of each window. It was much bigger and nicer than my own house. It had an upstairs, a downstairs, and a covered veranda on the front where you could sit and watch 5 After the Storm folks going by. An attached shed behind the house led to a large, faded red barn.

When she took me upstairs that first time, Aunt Rebecca showed me a room at the front of the house. "This was your mother's bedroom when she was growing up," she told me, "and now it is yours."

Aunt Rebecca gave me a few items that had belonged to Mama: a favorite wool shawl that still carried her scent, a small locket that she always wore that contained a tiny photo of Papa, and a small daguerreotype in a frame of Mama and Papa on their wedding day. I placed the wedding portrait on the little table beside my bed, and sometimes I would talk to Mama for a while before I fell asleep. I often wrapped myself in the shawl, even when it was not chilly. These things helped me feel closer to my mother, and a little bit less lonely, but I was still confused about what would happen when she came back to get me.

Aunt Rebecca was quite tall—of course, everyone is tall when you are a little girl—and stood up very straight. She always wore dark dresses with high necks and long sleeves, even in summer, and she pulled her dark hair back severely in a knot at the back of her head. Her face was quite pale, and she did not smile often, but when she did smile, her features softened. I wished she would smile more often.

In the first few weeks that I was in that house, I asked my aunt several times when I would see my mother again. "Will she take me back to the farm to live when she comes to get me, or will we live here?" Eventually, when my aunt could not give me a good answer, I stopped asking.

I missed Mama very much. I was often scared at night, all alone in the dark. I tried to be quiet, but Aunt Rebecca could hear my sobs and would come and sit by my bed and hold my hands until I fell asleep. Sometimes she would sing softly to me or tell me a story, and then I did not feel so scared.

I remember two recurring nightmares that started about that time and haunted me during most of my childhood. In one, I was falling endlessly through dark clouds with nothing to catch hold of to anchor me. All around me was rain, flashes of lightning, and the booming sounds of thunder. In the other dream, I was in a tunnel that was just big enough for my small body to crawl through. There was a dim light, so I could see that there was no end to it, no way out. Often, I woke up screaming for Mama and drenched in a cold sweat after one of these dreams. My aunt would come quickly to reassure me. "Nothing can harm you here," she used to say, and then she would stay with me until I went back to sleep.

After Aunt Rebecca helped me settle in the house, she introduced me to the chickens running around behind the house and to the two goats, Nellie, and Nora. I also met her large gray horse, a sweet-tempered mare named Jewel. She pulled Aunt Rebecca's wagon and my aunt allowed me to sit on her back sometimes as a special treat.

"Jewel has a baby every year or two," my aunt told me. "When you are old enough, you may have one of her babies for your own to raise."

"Oh, may I?" I said, clapping my hands with glee. "Oh, thank you!" I could hardly wait to meet my very own baby horse.

My aunt gave me a tour of her large vegetable garden and the barn and showed me where the privy was at the back of the shed, which connected the house with the barn. It was a "two-seater" though I could never imagine two people wanting to pee together! Thank goodness, I had a pretty chamber pot in my bedroom, so I did not have to go all the way out there in the dark in the middle of the night. Who knows what scary creatures might be lurking out there. It was my responsibility, young as I was, to empty and clean my chamber pot every morning.

There were chores to do every day and my aunt showed me how to collect the eggs from the chicken yard and sweep the kitchen floor. I also helped gather kindling for the big cast iron cooking stove in the kitchen and other tasks, as I was able. My aunt had a part-time hired man named Mr. Blackwell who took care of Jewel and the goats and brought fresh goat's milk to the kitchen door every morning. He also cut and baled hay in the fall, storing it in the hayloft to pitch down to the animals during the winter. The rest of the year, Jewel, and the goats ate fresh grass in the fenced-in fields behind the barn. The goats liked to come over and nuzzle my hand sometimes, through the fence, and Jewel, too. I learned to carry carrots or pieces of apple with me.

The first spring I was there, three baby goats were born. They were very playful and liked to jump and run around in the barnyard and butt heads with each other. I used to run along the fence and giggle at their antics. I was sad when my aunt sold them when they got older. I decided that someday I would have goats of my very own and never sell them.

Aunt Rebecca's house was at the edge of the village, the last one on the main street before the land turned into farmland, orchards and then to forest. Another road turned south just past our house. A beautiful lake was not far away—I could just see it from the windows in my bedroom. It was so big I could not see the far end and when the sun was shining, the surface of the water flashed and sparkled like a multitude of broken mirrors. I found the sight very soothing, almost hypnotic, and I would sometimes stand at the window for a long time on sunny days just staring at the sparkling water.

The stagecoach went right by our house several times each day along with farmers driving wagons or on horseback as they came to and from the village. On market days, many folks came to town in wagons and buggies, whole families sometimes. It was amazing to me that there were so many people coming to our little village. Market Day quickly became my favorite day of the month.

The center of the village was just a short walk down the road from our house. There was a general store right next to the lakeshore and the town beach, where Aunt Rebecca purchased things she needed for the house (or, more often, bartered in exchange for eggs or homemade jams and fresh baked goods). A pretty bandstand stood nearby on the other side of the town beach. A church stood on a little rise on the opposite side of the main street just beyond the one-room schoolhouse. There were other houses beyond the church and several small establishments—I remember a blacksmith shop, a telegraph and post office, and a shoemaker's shop.

It was all so different from my old home, which seemed isolated by comparison. I loved the hustle and bustle and seeing many people passing by our house or shopping in the village. However, I was shy and felt embarrassed when my aunt introduced me to her friends, neighbors, and shopkeepers. I grew hot and flustered, unable to do more than mumble a greeting. My aunt teased me a little about how red my face would get and how I looked at the ground instead of up at the person we were meeting, but she understood my discomfort.

"It must be difficult for you to meet so many new people, all at once," she said. "It will get easier with time." I hoped she was right.

Sometimes, when she took me with her shopping, I could see the expression on people's faces when they looked at me. Most seemed kind and welcomed me to the village but sometimes I could hear them whisper words behind us like "poor little orphan" as we walked down the street.

"What is an orphan?" I asked my aunt. "An orphan," she explained gently, "Is somebody who does not have a mama or a papa. Someone like you. Don't you pay them any mind. They mean no harm. Besides," she continued, "you have me now, and soon you will have lots of friends of your own to keep you company."

I began to notice a change in Aunt Rebecca from when I first came. She seemed more relaxed. The lines in her face softened and she moved with a lighter step. I even noticed that she smiled more than when I first arrived. My aunt was so thoughtful and loving that I began, eventually, to think of her as my mother, and she told me often she was glad that I had come. The first time she said that I pressed my face against her warm body and hugged her. I had no words for how I felt.

Chapter Two

My aunt was a dressmaker and an exceptionally good one, I learned, as I grew older. She introduced me to sewing right away. She gave me scraps from her dressmaking and showed me, with great patience, how to sew the pieces together with a needle and thread to make coverlets for my doll's bed. She also taught me to sew dresses and later fancy outfits for my doll, sometimes from scraps of silk or brocade but more often from cotton muslin and calicoes of different colors. Sometimes she would give me a snippet of lace to trim a tiny bonnet or petticoat hem.

How I loved those little scraps of fabric and the hours I spent with Aunt Rebecca, trying so hard to make my stitches as small as she said I should. I loved the feel of the fabric between my fingers, the colors, and the patterns I was able to make with only a little help.

I was in awe of Aunt Rebecca's beautiful treadle sewing machine and the marvelous dresses, cloaks, and pretty undergarments she created for her customers. Sometimes she would allow me to work the treadle for her as she sewed. As my legs grew long enough to reach the treadle, my Aunt would allow me to try out her beautiful machine if I promised to be especially careful. I remember vowing with all my heart,

"Someday I am going to have a beautiful sewing machine just like Aunt Rebecca's!"

That first spring, when I was not quite five, my aunt also showed me how to put seeds in furrows in the garden. She taught me the names of each flower and vegetable as it sent up a small green shoot, and I watched with fascination, as each tiny plant grew bigger. I made a promise to myself that I would not forget the names she taught me, and I never did! My aunt also planted many sunflowers at the back of the garden. They grew taller than I was. When the flowers dried in the fall, she put some of the flower heads in the yard for the chickens and other birds to feast on, shelled some of the seeds for us as a treat, and saved the rest for next year's garden.

Aunt Rebecca also had a large flower garden with plants that came back every year without having to plant new ones. She called them perennials. So many beautiful colors as each variety came into bloom. We had fresh cut flowers on the dining room table and on a small table in the parlor all summer long. The whole house smelled wonderful with their scent.

As I got older, I began asking Aunt Rebecca about my mother again. I did not remember my father at all but if I tried hard, I could still see my mother's long blond hair and her faded yellow dress. In my mind, she always seemed sad.

"What was my mother like, Aunt Rebecca?" I asked one day when we were in the kitchen. She sat me down on a stool while she kneaded dough for oatmeal bread and prepared apples for a pie.

"Caroline was a beauty when she was young," my aunt told me. "Eleven years separated her and me and sometimes I felt more like her mother than her sister. I had twin brothers a few years younger than me as well, Charlie and Victor. Their birthing was difficult for Mama and she almost died bringing them into this world. It took her a long time to recover, and she lost several babies after that. When she got pregnant with your mama, it was like a miracle and she took great care to keep her baby safe.

Papa was happy when the boys arrived, but he was also upset over how close he had come to losing Mama because of them. He adored Mama even though he was not good at showing it. From the first, he was hard on the twins and they, in turn, apparently enjoyed teasing him and egging him on. It seems they were always getting into trouble, even as little ones. They were about seven when you were born."

"Did my mama get in trouble when she was little?" I asked, curious. "Not like her brothers. She was a happy child, always laughing. She loved playing games, but she hated doing chores. I think she must have been my parents' favorite because she often got out of having to weed the garden or help with feeding the chickens or milking the goats, chores that ended up being left to me."

"I do chores. Why did you have to do Mama's share?" I asked.

"I guess it was just easier for me to do what needed to be done and let Caroline play. Caroline was the 'golden' child who could do no wrong! I was jealous and thought she was quite spoiled, but I also loved her. How could I not? She was so pretty, with her long blond hair and she lit up any room she entered!"

As she rolled out piecrust, my aunt continued, "My parents, (your grandparents), were pious, upright folks, and dedicated to our church. Pa was a lawyer. He made a comfortable living riding from town to town taking care of legal settlements such as boundary disputes and occasionally something more interesting. He had this house built when he and mama were first married."

"Riding from town to town sounds like fun," I said.

"I suppose he did not think so. Pa was a difficult man when we were growing up, much set in his ways, and far too fond of whiskey. Mama generally took his side in things. Disagreeing with him when he had made up his mind only led to angry words between them, and Pa would retreat into one of his black moods. She knew when to keep her thoughts to herself. Mama had a soft nature as well though she dared not show it when Pa was angry. She let us know, in quiet ways, that she sympathized with us on some issue, but made it clear that Pa must never know."

"Your Mama must have been a kind lady," I said. "Did she ever know me when I was very little?"

"Your grandma was a wonderfully kind and warm-hearted person. She would have loved you dearly, I am sure, just as much as she loved Caroline, but she died before you were born. You have your grandmother's name, you know. Your mama named you for me, as well, so you are Hannah Rebecca. I was deeply touched."

"I wish I had a grandma. Do you miss her? Do you miss my mama?"

"Yes. I miss your grandma very much and I miss Caroline more than I can say, my brothers, too. Every day something reminds me of what I have lost. I wish, sometimes, that things could have been different but there is no use fretting over things that can't be changed," Aunt Rebecca said softly. She composed herself then continued in a stronger voice.

"Mama was an excellent needlewoman and a weaver. She spun wool and flax on her tall spinning wheel that stood right here in this kitchen, and then she wove the fabric with which to make all our clothes and linens. There used to be a loom in the shed where she worked in summer. It was too cold to weave in winter."

"Do you know how to spin and weave cloth? Did my Mama learn how?" I asked.

"Your grandma taught me how, but your mother did not want to learn. We are fortunate these days. We can purchase whatever cloth we need at the general store and not have to make it ourselves."

"Who taught you to sew?" I asked.

"I learned from Ma," my aunt said, "just as you

are beginning to learn from me. She taught me to sew and embroider as well as to cook when I was about your age. She also taught me to be humble and not seek to better myself among my peers. I still have the sampler that I embroidered when I was eleven, and in spite of what Mama said, I was very pleased with the result! Would you like to see it? I have it in a frame in my room."

"I would like that," I said.

"We can see it after supper when we are not so busy."

I loved the smells of cooking in Aunt Rebecca's big kitchen. As we talked that day, the smells of baking bread and apple pie wafted from the cast iron stove and steam rose from the big pot of chicken stew from last night's dinner.

My aunt continued talking about her family. "Ma loved each of her children very much, but I think she had a soft spot for the twins since they had cost her dearly when they were born. She tried to keep them out of Pa's way, but they were wild and rascally, and she could not protect them when Pa got angry. It was not unusual for him to take his belt to one or the other, sometimes both."

I shuddered at the thought of being beaten. "Did he ever hurt you or Mama? Or Grandma?"

"No!" she said quickly. "Thank goodness Pa

never raised a hand against your grandma or my sister and I learned when I was young to stay out of his way. Pa was a religious man and strict with his children, except for Caroline. He read from the Bible every night and required each of us to read a passage aloud as well before he sent us off to bed. Since I was the oldest, I learned to be responsible, to do what Pa told me, and not speak out of turn. My brothers, on the other hand, were hot-headed and constantly butted up against Pa's rules. I think they enjoyed getting him riled up. I felt sorry for Charlie and Victor sometimes, but also felt they brought Pa's anger on themselves. As they got older, Pa's rages against them grew worse. It did not take much to get him going.

"Once, when the boys were washing up before dinner, I caught a glimpse of red welts and old scar tissue on Charlie's back. It made me sick. Our favorite days were when Pa was away on his lawyer business. Sometimes he would be gone for several days and we could all relax and be happy. However, we had to keep a lookout so we would know when he was coming back, and we always watched to see what mood he might be in when he got here. Sometimes he would come home bearing a small gift for Mama or a sweet for us, but more often than not, he would be surly and smell of whiskey. It was as if we were walking on eggs and had to be extra careful not to break any.

"Why did he drink so much?' I asked. "And why was he so mean?"

"I have always thought he must have been a very unhappy man. Perhaps his own father treated him that way. On the other hand, maybe that was just the way he was. No one really knew." Aunt Rebecca looked away. She put a hand to her face and brushed away a tear. Then she went on.

"Late one afternoon, when Vic and Charlie were about seventeen and Caroline was ten, Pa came home very drunk and went after the boys in a terrible rage. They were out in the barn taking care of the horses when he came after them, shouting curses. Charlie and Vic had grown tall and strong by then and I guess something must have snapped in them that evening. Together they were able to knock Pa unconscious and they left him lying in one of the horse stalls face down in the filth. Before Pa could come to, they took our two horses, a couple of blankets, and some food and took off, leaving only a brief note for Mama and me. They said they were headed west to seek their fortune and they would write when they could."

Aunt Rebecca stood quietly for a moment, remembering.

"The two of them leaving like that nearly broke my heart and Ma's too, but I also knew that life at home could not continue as it had been. We never saw either of them again but did receive a handful of letters over the next few years. We learned they had tried panning for gold and driving cattle, but not much more than that. Pa had a flattened nose, cracked jaw, and a black eye as a souvenir. He cursed the twins daily for running off with his horses and other gear, but I do not believe he ever understood why Charlie and Victor left home."

Rebecca took the bread and pies out of the oven and cut a generous slice of the fragrant bread for each of us covering them with some of my favorite strawberry jam.

"How did my Mama and Papa meet?" I asked, hoping Aunt Rebecca would tell me more.

"A few years after my brothers ran off, Caroline met a handsome young man named Jacob Applegate at a barn dance in the village. She was about fifteen then and a real beauty. Jacob came from the far side of Tamworth with his family to bring their timber and other farm goods to market day and they stayed for the evening festivities. Apparently, Caroline caught Jacob's eye that night, and he began to find ways to visit her whenever he could. Your grandfather forbade Caroline from seeing him, but they married in secret the following year when she was sixteen and he was twenty-two. His parents gave them some money and some livestock, and they rented a small farm about five miles outside the village, the one where you were born. Your Mama had a stillborn child less than five months after they married."

"Mama was very young then, wasn't she?"

"Yes, too young. Pa disowned her when he learned what she had done. He did not want to have anything to do with his new son-in-law, and would not allow your Grandma to visit Caroline, even after she lost the baby. I snuck over to see her when I could.

"What does 'disown' mean?"

"It means treating someone in your family as if they no longer exist. According to Pa, your Mama was no longer any part of his family. Your Grandma was terribly upset but she did not have the courage to go against Pa. A few weeks later, she tripped and fell, breaking her hip while carrying a pail of milk from the barn to the house. She was in agony. The doctor gave her laudanum, but it did nothing more than dull the pain. I guess, with everything that had happened, she lost her will to live and she slipped away from us, in spite of all we tried to do for her."

"I wish grandma was still here so I could meet her," I said, "and Mama too. It seems so unfair!"

"Life is not fair, my dear," Aunt Rebecca said. "You have to take the bitter with the sweet and make out as best you can." She had a faraway look in her eyes, remembering. "Pa drank more and more whiskey after Ma died and his black moods were constantly with him. I ran the household all by myself." Aunt Rebecca's face twisted in bitterness and pain.

"How old was my Mama when I was born?" I asked, trying to change the subject.

"She was almost twenty-four. The marriage did not turn out the way most of us hoped though your Mama was still crazy about your Papa. They did not have an easy time. Caroline never did learn the skills needed to run a household before she married and muddled along the best she could afterward. I even had to teach her how to kill and pluck a chicken for the stewpot and how to plant a successful garden, among other things. After several miscarriages, your Mama finally brought a new baby into the world, a boy, but he was sickly and did not live long. I could see that Caroline was beginning to lose heart and strength. She had become very thin, and her hair had lost its luster. She and Jacob both worked hard to keep the farm going but neither of them was really fit for farm life.

"When Caroline became pregnant again, I went to stay with her and Jacob in her last few months, and several neighbors came to lend a hand with the haying and other heavy chores. Sometimes their wives brought fresh baked bread or a casserole for us as well, so Caroline could rest as much as possible. Pa was furious when I told him I was going to stay with Caroline and help her with her baby, but this time I stood my ground. I would drive our wagon to my father's house once a day to cook his meals and tidy up, but that was all I was willing to do for him during that time. He was drunk most of the time anyway and hardly knew if it was day or night.

"When the baby finally arrived one hot August day, after a difficult birth, she was a beautiful, healthy blue-eyed girl. You! Your mother adored you and was truly happy for the first time in years. She slowly regained her health and I thought that finally, better times were ahead for your family. You were so sweet and smiled almost from the first. I can still remember how your little fingers curled around mine when I held you. You have always had a special place in my heart."

"What did Grandpa do after I was born?"

"I am afraid Pa never gave up his anger against your mother and would not visit, even after you were born. I offered to bring you to our house, but he refused. There is just no accounting for the anger and bitterness in some people." Something caught in her throat and she coughed. After a moment, she collected herself and continued.

"Caroline doted on you and your father did too. You were such a beautiful baby! I sewed a sweet set of baby clothes for you, buntings, and diapers, and I continued to visit two or three times a week. I could not stay away! You and your Mama both seemed to thrive which made me happier than I had been in a long time."

I loved hearing about Mama. I would beg for more stories about what she was like as a child and my Aunt Rebecca never seemed to tire of talking about her. Some days she gave me a dust rag and together we would go from room to room tidying up and dusting while she talked. Her stories made me feel closer to Mama, but I was sad too. I thought Mama could not have had a happy life after she grew up, or my Aunt Rebecca, as I began to understand.

I did not remember my papa at all and had often been curious to learn more about him but was afraid to ask. No one ever talked about him. One day, when we were in the garden weeding, I screwed up my courage and asked my aunt, "What can you tell me about my Papa? Why have I not heard anything about him?"

"He was a very handsome man and came from a good family on the far side of Tamworth. He cut a dashing figure at the time the two of them first met. All the older girls in the village wanted to dance with him at that barn dance, and he clearly enjoyed the attention! I can see why your mama fell so hard for him. As I recall, he was the youngest son of a large family with few prospects and not much ambition. Nevertheless, he had a big heart and was well intentioned. Looking back, I would say he was ill prepared for the life he chose. It was a great struggle to keep the farm going with just the two of them, and there was no money to hire help."

She straightened her back, resting for a moment. "I think that when the war came, it probably gave him an excuse to leave. He signed up as soon as the call went out and left with a regiment from the surrounding towns when you were about two and a half. Then he went and got himself killed six months later, down in Tennessee, or so we were told. His body was never found" my aunt said, her voice tinged with bitterness. "I suspect he might never have returned home, even if he had lived. I heard about many young farm boys who never returned home once they saw the larger world beyond New Hampshire."

Her words had stung me. "Aunt Rebecca," I said. "How could he leave us like that? Didn't he love Mama and me?" I burst into tears.

"Oh, Dear One, I am so sorry. I should not have said that. All I know is that he joined the army willingly and never came home. I still blame him for your mama's death that is all. It is my own bitterness talking. I didn't mean to hurt you." Aunt Rebecca knelt in front of me and held me close.

"Your papa did love you and your mama. I promise you that. You must understand, Hannah, it was a terrible time, everywhere, when the war started. Many men left their homes and families to fight to save their country from breaking apart. They felt it was their duty. Now many young men are dying or coming home with grievous wounds. It has been particularly difficult in small villages like ours with so many men gone away, and for women like your Mama, left alone with little ones to look after and a farm to run. I think your Mama just gave up when she heard that the love of her life was dead. When a fever came through the area not long after, she succumbed to it quickly. Many folks said, in later years that your Mama died of a broken heart. I think I felt the same. You were not quite four then. And that is how you came to live with me."

She looked at me, searchingly.

"Hannah, do you remember when first I brought you here?" I nodded. "My, how you screamed. Poor thing, you were terrified. I remember it was raining so hard we were both soaked through by the time I brought you home." She was silent for a moment, remembering. "I hope you are happier, now that you have been here a while."

"Yes, Aunt Rebecca. I truly am." I meant what I said, but I missed my mama more than ever.

Aunt Rebecca rarely spoke about herself and I was curious to know more about her. One day, while we were picking raspberries and blackberries behind the barn, I gathered my courage once again and asked,

"All the other ladies we know have husbands. Why don't you?"

"My, what a question, child!" she responded. Then more gently, she said, "I was not a beauty like your mother was, and I never met a young man whom I fancied enough to marry. Unlike your Mama, I enjoyed working hard and I stayed on in this house to look after my father after my mother died. I felt it was my duty and my cross to bear. By the time he died, I was no longer a young woman."

A shadow passed over her face and then she said softly, "You have to make the best of what you have been given in this life. Now shoo, no more questions today! Go and fetch the eggs from the chicken yard."

Apparently, my questions were never ending. Aunt Rebecca often teased me because my need to know everything was apparently insatiable! I decided I should wait a few days before I pressed my aunt for more information.

We were in her sewing room on a rainy afternoon, and she was making me a new dress to replace the one I had outgrown. This one was blue, my favorite color. I could not wait to try it on.

"You certainly are growing fast, my dear. I can hardly keep up with you! I think you may be tall someday like your father was. Here, hold still while I pin the hem."

"When did you learn to make dresses?" I asked.

"Goodness, you have so many questions! Well, I had a friend, Emily, whose parents worked at the general store. That was before the current owners, Mr. and Mrs. McNally bought it. Emily was a seamstress. She taught me all about the different types of fabric the store sold and how to follow a dress pattern. I began making dresses for myself, all by hand of course, and then for some for my friends. I guess word must have gotten around because soon other women in the village were asking me to make dresses and other items of clothing for them. I loved working with beautiful fabrics to make outfits and actually getting paid for it!'

"What did grandpa think about that?" I asked.

"Pa was not happy about what I was doing—he called it the devil's work, making fancy clothes, and putting on airs. However, I loved my work, and it was my income paying most of the bills, so he let me be. I purchased a beautiful treadle sewing machine just before you came to live with me and set myself up in business. That was unusual then. Women were expected to marry and take care of the children and household. If they did not marry, they were expected to stay home and take care of their aging parents. Well, I did what was expected of me and started a business, though, as you can see, it has not been easy." I nodded.

"Eventually, Pa's drinking was the end of him. The two of us had to do all the chores with Ma gone, in addition to my work as a seamstress. One day Pa was in the haymow high up in the barn, pitching hay down with a pitchfork. He was stinking drunk. I was feeding the goats below him and saw him stagger. Then suddenly, with one mighty heave of the pitchfork, he followed the hay and the pitchfork all the way down to the barn floor and broke his neck. I can't say I was sorry he was gone, and I did not mourn."

"And so, you lived here all alone after that?" I asked, not knowing what else to say.

"Yes," she said. "I loved my work and the freedom to live my life the way I wanted to after Pa died. Soon I began to make enough money to support myself. If I had married like my sister, I most likely would never have been able to do this. I like my life just the way it is, now." Then she added with feeling, "Of course, my life is so much richer with you here. You are the daughter I never had!" She gave me a big hug and I swelled up with happiness. I will never forget how her words made me feel.

I was much older before I fully understand why Aunt Rebecca felt so much bitterness. I knew what loss felt like, and Aunt Rebecca had lost both her brothers, her mother, her beloved sister and continued to care for a father she hated until she lost him too. She sacrificed her youth for her family without thanks and never married. At least, she had her parents' house and her fledgling business. Now, she had me.

One Sunday, after the church service was over, Aunt Rebecca took me by the hand and said, "There is someone I would like to visit, and I want you to come with me. I think it is time."

"Who?" I asked.

"You will see." Instead of walking towards the busy street where people were talking together in groups, or drifting off towards home, we walked towards the graveyard to the west of the church. As we passed through the small gate in the wrought-iron fence, I wondered, why would we be visiting anybody in a graveyard?

Aunt Rebecca walked beside me up a gently sloping hill towards the back of the cemetery, still holding my hand. Ahead of us was a small, carefully tended garden, where flowers bloomed yellow, white, and red. A weeping willow stood nearby. It felt peaceful. We stopped in front of a row of small stones lying in front of two larger stones that had words on them. "What do the words say," I asked.

"It says 'Here lies Charles Ira Horner, born in the year of our Lord, 1802, died 1860. RIP'. This one, next to it says 'Here lies Hannah Caroline Jackson, faithful wife of Charles Ira Horner, born in the year of our Lord 1805, died 1859. RIP.'" Aunt Rebecca knelt beside me. "This is my Ma and my Pa, your grandparents."

"What does RIP mean?"

"It means 'Rest in Peace'."

"This is where they live?" I asked in horror.

"This is where their bodies lie. Their souls are in Heaven," my aunt tried to explain. "These small stones are in memory of my brothers who left long ago."

"And this stone here? Is this one for my mama?" I was very confused.

"You know that your Mama is in Heaven, but her body lies here, with her family. Her stone says, 'Here lies Caroline Rachel Horner, loving wife of Jacob Applegate, 1834-1862'. You can come and visit her whenever you want to."

"Mama is never going to come for me, is she?" I said, a sob catching in my throat.

"No, dear one, she is not, I am so sorry."

This final proof was just too hard, and I sank into my Aunt's arms while tears streamed down my cheeks. Later I felt better, and I was glad that I had come to "visit" the stones. As we walked slowly back down the hill, the lake glittered in the sunshine below us. My world was beginning to make more sense to me.

Chapter Three

In the fall after I turned six, there was a long period of very wet and cold weather. With no one in the house but us, Aunt Rebecca and I brought in many armloads of firewood for the stove in the kitchen and the parlor fireplace. The dampness penetrated everything, even our bones, or so it seemed. One day, Aunt Rebecca developed a cough that got worse over the next few days. Her face looked flushed, and her skin felt very warm. She took to her bed, saying she just needed a little rest.

The following morning the house was quiet. I heard no coughing. Hoping she might be feeling better, I tiptoed into her room. My aunt's face was white; her dark hair was damp and matted against her forehead. Frightened, I called her name.

"Aunt Rebecca, wake up," I said. She did not respond. I took one of her hands and it was limp. I started crying. "Aunt Rebecca don't leave me," I wailed. I began to panic, terrified I would be all alone again. Without thinking, I ran down the stairs and out of the house into the pouring rain and continued as fast as my legs would take me to the general store, which was the closest place to our house.

I burst through the door into the warmth of the main shop room, dripping wet and crying. Mrs. McNally saw me and quickly came from behind the counter.

"Lord, child, what is the matter?" she asked.

"I'm so scared, Missus. I don't know what to do," I said through my tears. I was shaking.

"Tell me what has scared you, honey."

"My Aunt Rebecca—she is so sick. I could not wake her up this morning."

Mrs. McNally took off her apron and got her cloak. "You stay right here, Hannah. I am going to fetch the doctor." She went quickly into the back room to alert her husband and then ran to Dr. Jessup's house. Mr. McNally appeared with a big towel and dried me off as best he could then wrapped me in an old coat. He picked me up, carried me back to my aunt's warm kitchen.

"Don't you worry yourself none," he said as he was leaving. "Your aunt will be in good hands when the doctor comes." Then he ran back to the store to look after his own little girl.

Dr. Jessup arrived soon after with Mrs. McNally, and quickly went upstairs to my aunt's room. I ran after them.

"Is she going to die?" I asked, sobbing. Mrs. McNally put her arm around my shoulder. "Let's go down to the kitchen and make some nice hot tea and let the doctor take care of your aunt. I am sure he will know just what to do. And we need to get you into some dry clothes."

That day passed slowly, and I was still frightened. I could hardly sit still for worry. Mrs. McNally was kind and helped me feel a little bit better. In the late afternoon, Dr. Jessup came downstairs.

"Your aunt is going to be all right," he said gently. "She has pneumonia but should recover. In the meantime, we want her to drink lots of tea and to eat a little if she can. Mrs. McNally, perhaps you can make some soup. I will send my wife over to stay with Hannah tonight and to keep an eye on Rebecca. I will stop by later this evening and again tomorrow." He knelt down in front of me and said, "You are a very brave girl, Hannah. If you had not run for help, your aunt might not have made it this far. I think you may have saved her life!" He gave me a hug and left.

I ran upstairs as quickly as I could and went into Aunt Rebecca's room. She was lying back on her pillows, but her eyes were open.

"Oh, Aunt Rebecca—I thought I was going to lose you! I wouldn't be able to bear it if you were gone and I was left alone again!" I hugged her and cried tears of relief on her shoulder.

"There, there," my aunt said, her voice weak. "The doctor told me I am going to be fine in no time. He also told me how brave you were to run through this terrible rain to get help for me. I am so grateful, Hannah, to have you in my life."

Sometimes, when I was waiting to fall asleep at night, I talked to Mama very softly so my Aunt would not hear. It had become something of a habit when I had something on my mind or was upset. After what happened to my aunt, I asked Mama "What will happen to me if my aunt does die, or she moves away or she just disappears?" That thought terrified me. Who would take care of me? Would I have to live all alone in this big creaky house? Would I have to go live with strangers? Perhaps I would go live with the McNally's over the general store. They were nice people, truly kind. That might not be so bad. They have a little girl about my age. I could work in the store to pay my keep ..." Mama was a patient listener and by the time I fell asleep that night I felt much better.

It was several weeks before my aunt was up and back to her old self. Mrs. McNally and Mrs. Jessup took turns staying with us during the day while she was recovering. They brought fresh bread or biscuits with them and made a hearty soup or stew with the vegetables harvested from our garden earlier in the fall. I felt proud to be able to help care for my aunt. I brought her tea or bowls of nourishing soup upstairs to her bedroom until she felt strong enough to come downstairs for her meals again.

Chapter Four

That same fall, I started attending the little one-room schoolhouse not far from where we lived. Aunt Rebecca walked me there the first few days but after that I walked y myself, feeling a bit scared but also very grown up to be allowed to do so. It was the oldest of several schools in our village and was quite small. A big pot-bellied stove stood in the center of the room to keep us warm in winter. The teacher expected every child to bring a small log or a bunch of kindling with them to school every day during the fall then the town provided a wagonload of dry logs before winter set in.

There were separate doors for the boys and the girls to enter the front of the school. I never understood why they had to have two—one door would have been plenty! The boys had to sit on one side of the room and the girls on the other. Each child had a piece of slate and chalk—we had no paper or books back then.

Miss Hastings was our teacher for most of the years I was at school. She was quite young when she first came to our village, perhaps twenty, and brand new to teaching. I learned later that Miss Hastings graduated from the Normal School at Bradford Academy in Massachusetts, west of Boston. She came to our village by answering an ad put out by the local school board. Bradford Academy was a very prestigious teaching college for women at that time and I imagine the school board expected a lot of our new teacher!

Miss Hastings appeared to be a bit nervous when we gathered in the little schoolhouse for the first time that fall. I liked her immediately. She was pretty and slim with curly brown hair coiled in a net at the back of her head and wearing a plain dark blue dress. She had a friendly smile for each of us and was quick to learn our names and ages. She was also quite strict. I guess she had to be to keep a room full of energetic children of different ages under control. It was not long before some of the older boys were vying for her attention, offering to clean the slate blackboard, or to carry her books home for her after school. I guess we all developed a kind of crush on her that first year!

Aunt Rebecca had already taught me my letters and numbers and I could read pretty well when I started school, so it was mostly easy for me in the beginning. To my delight, I discovered that I loved reading almost as much as I loved sewing! I had a harder time with numbers. When Miss Hastings asked if one person had three apples and another person had five apples, it was not too hard to figure out how many apples they had together. I could see the apples in my mind and count them. However, when she wrote the numbers on the board, they looked like hen scratching to me, and I was totally lost. I hated not knowing how to do it—I wanted to know how to do everything right away! One of the boys, not much older than I was, offered to help me when I couldn't solve a number problem. His name was Aaron. He had a quick mind and figuring out how things work (like math questions) came easily to him. I also learned he loved to read as much as I did.

After school, I did my chores, as usual, throwing down seed for the chickens who ran everywhere in the back yard and collecting eggs from under the bushes and tucked away in dark corners. When the leaves began to turn yellow and red and the temperature became nippy, we "put up" jar after jar of preserved or pickled vegetables, jams, and jellies. We hung onions and garlic by braided stems from rafters in the unheated pantry, along with a variety of herbs. Potatoes, winter squash, carrots, parsnips, and other root vegetables, as well as apples and jugs of fresh cider, went to the cellar to stay cold through the coming months.

On Saturdays, Aunt Rebecca would set up the large copper tub near the stove in the kitchen. We would then heat pots of water until we had enough to fill the tub. She helped me wash my long blond hair and scrubbed my back for me. Then I would help her wash her hair by pouring pitchers of water over her head. Sometimes we made a game of it and splashed each other until we both began to giggle and ended up with water all over the kitchen floor. That was the only time I ever heard Aunt Rebecca laugh.

The kitchen became my favorite room in the house. I learned how to cook simple dishes, how to bake bread and muffins, and how to make a flaky pie crust. Oh, the pies we made from the ripe berries—blueberries, black and red raspberries, apples with cinnamon. We sliced apples and other fruits, putting the slices on baking sheets in the oven to dry for winter pies, and stewed fruit to put up in jars. A large grapevine covered a trellis near the side of the house facing the barn. It had the sweetest grapes! We ate them fresh, made jelly, and dried a lot to make raisins. In the winter, I shelled the dried beans and helped cut up potatoes, onions, and carrots for flavorful and filling stews.

Most important of all these things, I learned how to sew. I learned how to hem linen napkins and tablecloths, how to crochet doilies from cotton thread, how to embroider lovely designs onto cotton handkerchiefs and eventually how to make some of my own clothes. When I was a bit older, I created my own sampler with all the letters of the alphabet and numbers laid out in tiny stitches. I embroidered a little white church with weeping willows on either side. Garlands of flowers wound around the borders. I completed it by stitching my name and the date, October 23, 1869. I was eleven. Aunt Rebecca was pleased when she saw my finished sampler and offered to have it framed. We decided her sampler and mine should hang together in the parlor. I was thrilled.

Aunt Rebecca saved pictures of the many styles of dresses and other clothing from women's magazines, especially from Godey's Ladies Book, which had all the most current fashions. Some of them were very fancy and meant for society folk in the big cities. Aunt Rebecca was able to work out how to make patterns for simpler versions of these designs for her customers.

Her designs fascinated me with their intricate diagrams and cutting instructions. My aunt patiently taught me how to lay out the pattern pieces and fabric, and carefully cut each piece, marking the points at which they would fit together. It seemed almost like magic when she completed a dress for a customer:

so many ruffles and flounces, the lace, tiny buttons, and other decorative details. Of course, sometimes a customer wanted a beautiful bonnet and gloves to match the dress, sometimes even a parasol.

Although our village was small, Aunt Rebecca's reputation as a fine dressmaker had spread and wealthier people came from a distance to order dresses and accessories from her. I eventually learned to make simple dresses for myself but decided such fancy dressmaking was not for me.

Aunt Rebecca told me almost every day how proud she was of me, and sometimes she teased that I would make someone a wonderful wife before I reached the ripe old age of twelve. I blushed with pleasure when she said that.

Chapter Five

One day in April of 1865, when I was not quite seven, word came by telegraph that the war had ended! General Robert E. Lee had surrendered. Everyone cheered and waved flags and the church bells rang all over town. It was a great day. A few days later, terrible news reached our little village. Everyone cried, including my aunt.

"What has happened, Aunt Rebecca?" I asked. "Why is everyone so upset after being so happy just a few days ago?" It was very confusing.

"Someone has killed President Lincoln. He and Mrs. Lincoln went to see a play to celebrate the end of the war, and a man shot him, and he died."

Oh, it was a sad time. No one seemed to know what was going to happen. However, I was still young so after a while, I snuck off to play with some of the other children and tried to stay out of the way of the adults.

Not long after that, we received word that some

of the men who went away from our village and nearby towns were on their way home. That helped lift everyone's spirits. On a hot afternoon, a few days later, an officer rode into town on an enormous horse with a group of soldiers in uniform marching smartly behind him, kicking up dust on the road as they passed. The townsfolk gathered to welcome them, cheering as they marched by. The soldiers' uniforms were dirty and worn, even torn in places, but they stood tall and proud and waved back to the small crowd.

Then several wagons rolled through the center of town after the soldiers, and I saw men with bandaged legs or arms or with a bloody rag wound around their head. Behind those wagons came two more that were completely covered by blankets and flags.

The sounds of cheering died down. I heard gasps and exclamations from several people as the last wagons approached. The procession stopped in the center of town near the bandstand and the crowd moved toward them to greet the soldiers and look for loved ones. Mixed with the happy sounds of reunion were the sobs of women who found their husbands or sons grievously wounded or hidden in the last wagons.

It was not until I was much older that I understood just how significant that homecoming was. For those relatively few soldiers who returned whole, life gradually returned to what it had been before the war. However, many battle scars are not visible on the outside but hide deep within. Some soldiers never truly healed.

Those that returned with visible wounds had a long convalescence ahead of them. They returned to their former occupations when they could or found new ways to earn their living. For many wives, sisters and mothers, life could never be the same again.

Because of my own experience with death and grief, I felt great sympathy for our friends and neighbors who had lost someone or who was now caring for an invalid. Our elders kept my friends and me busy running errands or making deliveries of freshly baked bread or eggs and milk where the need was greatest. Still, we crept away to play when we could because the world of our elders seemed scary and sad.

CARY FLANAGAN

Chapter Six

I made friends at school in spite of my shyness. Of the eight girls and eight boys in our tiny school, two of the girls were about my age: Lydia and Jane. Lydia was a small child as I remember, shorter than I was and very thin, almost bony. She had dark hair that she wore in pigtails with the hair sticking out here and there. Lydia seemed more than just shy, and it took a while for her to warm up to me. She was jumpy and fearful of everyone, at first, especially the boys, yet she clearly wanted to be accepted. Gradually she seemed more comfortable in her new surroundings and more trusting of the other children and Miss Hastings.

I noticed that she always wore the same drab dress to school, and she did not look well cared for. I also noticed she never brought anything to eat for our midday break. I wondered why her mother did not help her get ready for school or send her with something to eat.

I began to share my sandwiches with Lydia at noon or gave her pieces of fruit or a muffin. I asked Aunt Rebecca for extra in my lunch so that I could share it. I just told Lydia that my aunt gave me more food than I could eat and that she would be doing me a favor by taking some of it. I could see that Lydia was embarrassed but she was also grateful.

Jane was quite the opposite. She was about my height, somewhat plump and nice looking, if not actually pretty. She had brown hair that she wore in ringlets down to her shoulders with a pretty ribbon to keep the curls off her face. She had two or three different dresses that she liked to wear, each with a matching ribbon, and she always looked and smelled clean. I can still remember her merry laugh—she was outgoing and seemed always to be in good humor. She, too, had extra food in her lunch pail that she gave to Lydia.

I was surprised when I discovered that Jane's parents owned the general store. I told her one day about how her mother and father had helped me to save my aunt's life. She said she had heard the story, and that her parents thought I was very brave. However, she did not know it had been me! Despite of our differences Lydia, Jane and I became fast friends.

The other girls in our school were older by several years and made fun of us sometimes. They especially teased Lydia because she never changed her dress or brought food for our noon break. I remember one girl named Charlotte and another Julia, and I think there was a girl named Anna, but I cannot remember the names of the other three. When they were cruel to Lydia, Jane and I always stood up for her.

Aaron, the boy who helped me with my numbers, was the youngest of four brothers in the school. Will was the oldest, then Jesse and Daniel. There were four other older boys. I think Samuel was the name of one of them and another was Oliver. All of them remained aloof, not wanting anyone to think they were sissies for paying attention to the "babies." I would have marveled if I had known then that the Benson brothers would one day become my family!

During the winter months, Aaron and his brothers often missed school because it was too far to walk from their house to the in the snow. They were also absent during haying season to help their father get the hay into the barn before the rains came and again when it came time to cut and stack enough firewood to last all winter. I missed Aaron on the days he did not come.

Occasionally my aunt allowed me to invite either Lydia or Jane to come home with me after school to have tea. Each girl always went home with a loaf of fresh baked bread, muffins, or a jar of jam. I really enjoyed these visits and gradually developed a sense of "belonging" among my schoolmates.

We were always busy at home, planting all manner of fruits, vegetables, and flowers in the spring, tending the gardens then preparing for winter by preserving and storing what we had grown to see us through the long cold season. We also took care of the large house and the chickens, goat, and Jewel, my aunt's horse (when Mr. Blackwell was not around). So many chores and things to do.

Nonetheless, we also had time to play. The children in my neighborhood enjoyed many outdoor games when the weather was fine and indoor games when it was rainy or snowing too heavily. In the heat of summer, our elders allowed us to swim in the lake.

There was a nice beach not too far from the center of town. The water there was shallow enough for young children to play (under the watchful eye of an adult). I was nervous about being in the water but did enjoy splashing about and getting wet in the hot weather. I never did learn how to swim and was jealous of the children who could.

Of course, there were festivities on the Fourth of July— a parade, a marching band, and a huge picnic on the village green. Everyone in town (or so it seemed to me) brought a dish to share and we ate until we almost burst! Then there was more music, and the grown-ups would dance. Later in the evening, there were fireworks bursting in a multitude of bright colors over the lake. What a sight!

In early October, there was a harvest festival combined with a large farmer's market. People came from the surrounding towns to sell their goods or to buy. There was always a potluck supper and a barn dance in the evening, just like the one where my mother and father first met.

The festivities at Christmas time were the best. Every building on the main street burned candles in their windows and hung pine and hemlock boughs on their doors. On Christmas Eve, after church, many folks gathered outdoors, near the church, to hold candles and sing carols. Each home and business opened their doors to the carolers, and we stopped to visit them and enjoy hot cider or cocoa and freshly baked cookies decorated for the holiday. At midnight, the church bells rang, and everyone returned home. It was a happy time and it made up for having to sit still in church most of Christmas Day. Aunt Rebecca always made a delicious

Christmas dinner after church and there was always a small gift for me, a doll she had made or a new dress and always a special sweet. I loved Christmas.

We played my favorite games in winter. If we were lucky, the lake would freeze over before the snows came, and we could skate for miles. We played tag or crack the whip and raced each other to see who was the fastest. One or another of Aaron's brothers usually won but I was almost able to keep up with them. I cannot remember anything as exhilarating as trying to outskate the boys! Sometimes, if we skated too far out on the lake, we could hear a deep booming noise under the ice, and we quickly skated closer to the shore, just in case.

Some of the men in town cut holes in the ice to fish. I thought it would be boring to sit waiting for a bite, but it was exciting when one of them landed a large bass or trout. One time a visiting fisherman caught a trout weighing more than ten-and-a-half pounds! He was proud of his catch and posed for a photograph with it.

Farther down the lake, a large storage building filled with sawdust sat beside the water's edge. Men went out on the ice to cut large chunks of ice with long saws that moved up and down. The ice could be as much as twenty-four inches thick and could support the weight of several adults. The chunks cut from the harvesting area were so huge teams of oxen had to haul them to shore. Then they were stored in the sawdust. My aunt took me there in the summer whenever we needed more ice for the chest in our pantry. The block was so heavy it was hard to carry so we chipped it down into convenient sizes. We brought the chunks home in the back of our wagon, wrapped in a blanket.

It was a treat to suck on the smaller ice chips on a hot day.

After a big snowstorm, men would hitch teams of oxen together and drive from one farmhouse to another then back to town to break out the roads. The older children took turns standing on the heavy wooden beam dragged behind the oxen to smooth out the trampled snow and ice. In later years, the road crews used a more efficient wooden snow roller that was four or five feet high and was hitched to a team of oxen or horses to flatten the snow. That road surface was perfect for running sleighs and horse races.

The most fun of all after a big snow was coasting or tobogganing down the hills around town. The Benson farm had the best hill for coasting—it was so long! I felt as if I could fly down it. There were many trees at the bottom, pines, and hemlock, so our elders warned us constantly not to crash into them at the bottom. When I finally went home, exhausted and freezing, there was always a roaring fire and hot cocoa waiting for me and the delicious feeling of snuggling into dry clothes.

Occasionally, when the weather was bad and my aunt did not need me, I enjoyed curling up in a corner of the parlor with a book. I loved how a good story transported me to another place and time, and I truly savored those rare moments when I just disappeared, visiting other countries, making new friends, and learning new and marvelous things.

Aunt Rebecca had a large collection of books in her parlor, and I devoured the novels, poetry, and even some of the books that were not fiction. Some of my favorite novels were by Charles Dickens and

Nathanial Hawthorne. I especially enjoyed the novels of Jane Austen and the Bronte sisters. I was thrilled that women had written such engaging stories and that they were so witty and smart.

My favorite of all was Little Women by Louisa May Alcott and learning about Jo March and her sisters. But then I also found myself feeling jealous that the March family had two loving parents, and a house full of happy sisters while I had only Aunt Rebecca. I told my aunt about all the wonderful places I had visited in my stories, who I "met," and what I had seen and learned, but I never mentioned wishing I had a father and mother like the March family.

I was happy in those days, most of the time. I still missed Mama, but my aunt seemed to know just what to say when I was feeling sad. She often told me I looked more and more like my mother every day, with my long blond hair, blue-gray eyes, and creamy skin. She enjoyed braiding my hair so that it hung in one long plait down my back. It was almost long enough to sit on now.

"I used to braid your mother's hair just this way when she was your age," she said, warmly. I think the only thing I wished for in those early years (besides having Mama back, of course), was a sister. How I longed to have a sister of my own! I remember asking my Aunt Rebecca once when I was little, if we could please get a little sister for me! She just hugged me and said she did not think that would be possible. It is funny, now that I think back, how our wishes may come true in ways we could never have imagined!

Chapter Seven

In the fall following my ninth birthday, when I had invited Lydia to visit, my aunt offered to make her a new dress. She told Lydia she had lots of fabric left over from her dressmaking and asked her to choose a color she liked.

"Oh, no, Miss Horner, I couldn't accept such a generous gift," She said she would get in trouble if she did.

"How could having a pretty new dress that costs nothing get you in trouble?" Aunt Rebecca asked her. Lydia looked at the floor and did not answer.

"How about this dark pink," my aunt said gently. "It goes nicely with your dark hair and will help bring color to your pretty cheeks. I can add a bit of lace if you want me to."

"Oh no," said Lydia, embarrassed. "It can't be fancy! I mean, for school." Lydia finally agreed to let my aunt make her a simple pink dress. I was so excited the day the dress was ready.

"May I bring Jane home with me for the fitting as well as Lydia?" I asked.

"That would be nice, dear. It will be fun."

Lydia was excited too. The look on her face when she put on the dress and saw herself in the mirror was priceless! She beamed, turning first one way, and then the other. I could have sworn that she had never seen herself in a mirror before.

Then Lydia said she did not want to wear the dress home and asked, hesitantly, if it might be all right to keep it at school. She said it would stay cleaner that way.

"But won't your parents enjoy seeing you in a new dress?" my aunt asked. "You look so nice in it. The color really suits you."

"It is just Pa and my baby sister and me at home," Lydia answered, dully. "This pretty dress will just get dirty there."

I did not understand at the time why wearing the dress home bothered Lydia so much, but I can remember the look on Aunt Rebecca's face when she said, very gently, "No matter, Lydia. I am sure Miss Hastings will not mind if you keep the dress at school. You can change into it for your classes, and you are always welcome to wear it here. Now change back into your own dress and run along home. Hannah can bring the new dress to school tomorrow."

It was not until I was much older that I found out how things stood at Lydia's house. Her mother had died in childbirth when Lydia was five. By some miracle, the baby, another girl, survived. Lydia finally named her Rose when her father did not 51 After the Storm come up with a better name than "brat". He barely took care of the two of them. Lydia fed the baby and tried to keep her clean. She always looked very tired and sad when she arrived at school in the morning, and always wore the same worn-out dress until she outgrew it and her father had to get her another one.

Hannah's Journal Inscription: This journal belongs to Hannah Rebecca Applegate, a gift from her Aunt Rebecca, on the occasion of her tenth birthday, August 27, 1868.

Dearest Mama, for I think I will use these pages to write to you and tell you about my life while you are far away from me in heaven. Aunt Rebecca gave me this little journal because she knows how much I love books. She suggested I write about my own thoughts and feelings and most especially, to record the many things for which I am grateful. She told me she had kept such a journal herself when she was my age and it gave her great pleasure to write in it when she was happy, and when she was feeling sad or angry it made her feel better to write down what was bothering her. It is one of my most treasured gifts. Therefore, dearest Mama, first I want to tell you how grateful I am to be living here with your dear sister. I was so young when you left us, but Aunt Rebecca took me in and she has loved me as her own all these years. She misses you too! She has told me all about you and Papa. Are you and Papa together again? Do you have the baby you lost? I often wonder what it must be like in Heaven. I hope you are happy there and that I will see you again someday. Aunt R. says you were very beautiful, and she thinks I will look just like you when I grow up. I hope so. She says I am a great help to her and that she is proud of me for learning so many new things. I think you would be proud of me too. I like school very much and have made some good friends. Miss Hastings is my teacher, and my two best friends are Jane and Lydia. They sometimes visit Aunt Rebecca and me after school. I still miss you every day, Mama, but lying in the bed you used to sleep in and talking to you in the dark comforts me. Sometimes I dream of you and then I feel as if you are with me in spirit while I sleep. Your loving daughter, Hannah

PS. My penmanship is not good yet, but I am working on it.

CARY FLANAGAN

Chapter Eight

One day, a few months after I turned eleven, Lydia's father, Mr. Murray, arrived at the school drunk in the middle of the day and demanded Lydia to come home at once.

"Yer sister is sick," he slurred. "Git back home where you belong and take care of her!"

Lydia was wearing another pretty dress that my Aunt had made for her since she had outgrown the first one by then. When her father saw the dress, he became angry. "Where in tarnation" (he used another really bad word) "did you get that dress? I ain't takin' no charity handouts from nobody! Yuh hear me?" Lydia cowered beside Miss Hastings and began to cry.

Miss Hastings spoke quietly to Will, the oldest of Aaron's brothers, and asked him to run quickly to find the doctor and the sheriff. While he was gone, Miss Hastings spoke calmly to Mr. Murray while the older boys in the class stood behind him in case he got out of hand. "What is the name of your little girl," she asked him.

"Just make Lydia come home 'n take care of her," he snarled.

"I am sure you are concerned about your daughter, Mr. Murray. What is the nature of her illness? We can send Dr. Jessup to your place to help her."

"Just give me Lydia!" he shouted, lurching unsteadily towards Lydia and Miss Hastings. Two of the boys caught his arms and held him. He struggled and tried to get away.

Will returned shortly with Dr. Jessup and Sheriff Peterson as well as a couple of other able-bodied men. They were able to calm Mr. Murray somewhat. As the men led him away, he yelled,

"Mark my words: yer goin' to pay for this! Someone is goin' to pay!" They took him off to the jailhouse to sober up. We heard him ranting about "vengeance shall be mine" all the way down the street.

I ran home to tell my aunt what had happened, and she came and fetched Lydia home with her. Lydia was as white as a sheet and still shaking when we got her home. Aunt Rebecca wrapped a blanket around her and held her until she calmed somewhat while I made a hot bath in the kitchen near the stove. Aunt Rebecca helped Lydia undress. What we both saw then was shocking. Dark bruises covered Lydia's arms and back. There were also bruises on her legs. My aunt tried to keep her features neutral and gave me a sign to do the same while we gently helped Lydia wash. It appeared as if she had not bathed for many months, and the whole time Lydia was in the tub, she cowered and shook.

I gave Lydia one of my nightgowns and we put her to bed to rest. My aunt whispered to me to keep an eye on her while she went to speak to Dr. Jessup. Aunt Rebecca told me later that Mrs. Peterson, the sheriff's wife, went with Miss Hastings and Dr. Jessup to the rough cabin in the woods where Lydia and little Rose lived with their Pa. What they found there horrified them, the filth, the lack of any proper sanitary facilities, dirty blankets on the floor for the girls to sleep on and hardly any food in the small pantry. They agreed it was time to find another home for the children if the selectmen would allow it.

Dr. Jessup wrapped little Rose in one of the blankets and carried her home with him to clean up and to give her proper medical care. He told us the next day she appeared to have pneumonia. Lydia stayed on with my Aunt and me and when Rose began to recover, Aunt Rebecca agreed to take Rose in as well. Later that month, the selectmen and church elders met and decreed that neither child should return to their father. The selectmen also agreed that the town should pay my aunt a generous stipend of $10.00 per month, more than enough to feed and support both children.

Eventually, the Sheriff sent Joseph Murray away to a larger jail in Concord after he tried to break into the general store looking for liquor. That time, he was even more combative than before, shouting,

"I swear on my dead wife's grave, someone will pay for this! Those girls are mine! They belong to me! I will come and claim them, you mark my words!"

The entire sad episode created quite a stir in town, with some folks thinking one way and some another.

Secretly, I was happy about how things turned out. I had my best friend living with me like a sister, and Rose was the little sister I always wanted. The two of them thrived under Aunt Rebecca's caring support and guidance, not to mention an abundance of good food. In this way, Lydia and Rose became a permanent part of our little household. We heard nothing from Mr. Murray for many years after that, and no one in town had any inclination to seek him out.

Journal Entry, May 1869

Dearest Mama — My heart is hurting for my best friend Lydia. I have just learned a hard lesson: there are some truly evil men in the world. Lydia's father is such a one. I hope never to see him again as long as I live! Aunt R. and I have agreed never to discuss what we witnessed when we saw the bruises on Lydia's body, but I feel such pain thinking about it. My sincere wish is that Lydia will be able to put this all behind her in time and learn to be happy again, now that she and her little sister Rose are safe. and living with us.

However, here is an irony, Mama: My wish to have a sister has come true! In fact, I now have two. Can you imagine? Therefore, I have also learned that much good can come from something evil. I am grateful for that.

Your hurting daughter, Hannah

It was not long before my aunt was teaching Lydia and Rose how to sew. Lydia took to sewing right away, just as I had. She loved planning how to make a dress, cutting and sewing the various parts of an outfit. With my aunt's assistance and encouragement, she made several dresses for herself and for Rose. She also learned how to make a simple quilt from Aunt Rebecca's scraps, and she and I made a game of seeing who could finish a quilt top first (all by hand, of course).

Rose, at almost six, could not seem to get her fingers coordinated for sewing. Even the simplest stitches were beyond her, and she often got very frustrated with trying. Nonetheless, she did love working in the garden and kitchen with Aunt Rebecca, and soon became an excellent helper.

Although they both seemed happy enough living with us, I would often wake at night, hearing Lydia cry out as if from a bad dream. I would go to her bedside to see what had scared her. Aunt Rebecca would hear her as well and would sit with her for a while, as she has done when I first came. Lydia seemed to carry a heavy weight everywhere she went. If I asked her what was bothering her, she would brush it off and say "nothing."

By contrast, Rose was a delight and hardly any darkness seemed to touch her. The only exception was that she seemed overly sensitive to any real or imagined criticism and was occasionally moody. The two sisters were close. Lydia was her little sister's caretaker and protector, although she eventually allowed these roles to devolve to Aunt Rebecca.

Gradually, Lydia became more relaxed and

comfortable in our home, and more confident. Whatever had happened to her before she came to live with us appeared to trouble her less, at least during the day. However, it was many years before her nightmares finally went away completely.

Lydia immersed herself in sewing with my aunt and eventually she became a skilled seamstress under Aunt Rebecca's careful tutelage. When she was seventeen, she became my aunt's official dressmaking assistant in return for her room, board, and a small salary. By then her "baby" sister, almost twelve had turned into a sweet though very shy young woman. As Rose grew older, she was a great help in preparing our meals and running the household. Eventually, Rose did most of the cooking and garden work while I continued to do most of the other chores so that Aunt Rebecca and Lydia could spend more time keeping up with the growing demand for Aunt Rebecca's dressmaking skills.

Chapter Nine

My friendship with Jane continued to grow during this time as well. Sometimes, Jane, Lydia and I stopped at her parents' general store on our way home from school to visit or to pick up something my aunt needed. Jane's mother always welcomed Lydia and me with a big smile and an offer of a sweet from one of the many jars on the counter (my favorite part of the store). She was very round and jolly, always talking and laughing with the customers. I do not think I ever saw her angry with anyone in all the years I knew her. Next to my aunt, she was my favorite adult while I was growing up. I will be forever grateful to her for what she did to help Aunt Rebecca and me when my aunt was so sick.

I did not see much of Jane's father. He was responsible for keeping the books and bringing in new stock. Occasionally, he appeared when I was there with an armload of shovels or a few bolts of new calicos. He also spent one or two days each week away from the store with a large "Tinker's" wagon. He would go from farm to farm in the outlying areas to sell his wares to folks who rarely came into town. He would collect from them fresh butter and milk, apples, furs, and wool in trade, or whatever else they might have, in season. When I saw him at the store, he always had an affectionate word for Jane, a warm greeting for me, and a smile for his wife but otherwise was quite reserved.

I marveled at the variety and abundance of wonderful things sold in the store. They had everything from giant pickles in a barrel to pitchforks and kerosene lamps, not to mention staples such as potatoes and baking flour, eggs, and fresh vegetables in season. I could see huge bags of grain for livestock, along with parasols and dress gloves of fine leather or lace. If you brought in your own jars or bottles, you could get honey or maple syrup measured out for you. There was not a single inch of space left unused in the entire store. It was almost more than a mind could take in.

Behind the counter was a shelf filled with bolts of fancy dress fabrics, including silks, satin and the more common muslins and calicos along with threads and notions of every kind and color imaginable! This shelf fascinated me, and I wished I could go behind the counter to get a closer look. There was also a giant wheel of the most delicious cheddar cheese next to the register, and you could ask to have a tiny piece cut off for a taste or a wedge wrapped in paper to take home.

Aunt Rebecca ran a tab at the general store that she would pay off at the end of each month with her hard-earned money. Often, she bartered fresh eggs or her own homemade jams or pies for part of what she purchased that month. Other folks in town did the same, bringing in fresh vegetables, bushel baskets of apples, jars of maple syrup from their own trees—

whatever they could barter. That is why there were always fresh goods at the store. It was an arrangement that worked well for everybody.

In summer, folks gathered on the wide veranda in front of the store to rest and gossip in the shade when they had the time. There was a swinging bench at one end of the veranda and several rocking chairs to the right of the entry into the store. Fresh lemonade or sarsaparilla with a chunk of ice was a welcome treat on a hot day!

In winter, men gathered around the big pot-bellied stove that stood in the center of the large main room and smoked their pipes or cigars and talked. The store was warm and welcoming and had a wonderful smell of pipe tobacco, spices, and herbs, fresh baked bread, and donuts. It seemed to me that this store was the very heart of the village. Except for my aunt's house, the general store was my favorite place to be!

Journal Entry: July 1869

Dearest Mama— So many things have happened in my life recently, but they are mostly good. I miss school now that it is summer. Miss Hastings was able to get a small supply of notebooks last winter and we spent the months before summer break practicing our penmanship by writing little stories. It was fun making up stories and writing them down. I have been writing more this summer. I think I am getting better at it! Miss Hastings has loaned Lydia and me some books to read over the summer. I am currently reading Pride and Prejudice by Jane Austen, which Aunt Rebecca does not have in her library. I am enjoying learning about the different social customs in England. It is also interesting to see how pride can get in the way of happiness. It is a wonderful story, and I am pleased that a woman wrote it!

I am grateful for my friends for helping me feel more confident and less shy, especially Jane, who is so outgoing and loves to talk, the way her mother does. She makes me laugh with her silly jokes and sense of fun. The only thing that bothers me right now is that Lydia still has nightmares and seems nervous around most people. We do not talk about it, but I wish we could. It is a shadow over her that I wish would go away. I thought she might enjoy reading about the March family in Little Women, but I fear it may have had the opposite effect in reminding her of what she does not have. I feel sad that I cannot help her.

Your loving daughter, Hannah

Chapter Ten

Aunt Rebecca accompanied the three of us to the village church every Sunday. Almost everyone in town attended but Aunt Rebecca confided to me years later she only went to church because it would not look right if she did not go and because she felt it was important for us to attend. Of course, I never told anyone that!

I always went with her from the first Sunday I lived with her. When I was little the pastor of our church scared me. He had a full black beard, bushy eyebrows, and wild eyes. He appeared to be angry all the time, frowning and sometimes shouting at the people who listened to his sermons. Apparently, he thought that everyone would burn in hell unless he or she was perfect in this life. He made me cry sometimes. I was happy when he retired, and a much younger pastor took over.

The new pastor, Pastor Isaiah Stevens was much friendlier and more approachable than our old pastor was. He smiled at everyone who came into his church, tipped his hat, nodded to the women, and shook hands with the men. No one seemed to know much about where he came from or what his experience was in the church. However, he was so likable and put everyone at ease with his friendly manner, no one questioned his background.

Pastor Stevens had some new ideas about God and religion. He did not believe everyone would automatically burn in hell. In fact, he believed in salvation and a kinder, more forgiving God. I came to enjoy his sermons and I think most everyone else felt the same way (even my aunt). The part of the church service I enjoyed most was the singing. The old pastor had us singing mournful hymns, but the new pastor picked out hymns that had beautiful melodies and uplifting words, and I often felt joyful after the service. I began to notice a change in the way other people looked and acted while leaving church services. There was a lighter mood, and townsfolk stopped to visit with one another more often after the service than in the past.

Pastor Stevens visited the families in the village and outlying farms to get to know them better and see to their needs. He apparently did not have a family of his own and I think he enjoyed the warm reception and hospitality he received from most of the families he visited. (The story was that he had had a young wife who died in childbirth some years before. However, he never spoke of it and everyone respected his privacy on that matter).

The first time he visited with us, Aunt Rebecca and Rose fluttered about, making sure to use the best china for tea and to lay out the freshest biscuits and cookies while Lydia and I kept him company in the parlor. He seemed interested in our little "family" and asked us many questions. He told me how sorry he was about the loss of my parents and the circumstances that had brought Lydia and Rose to live with us.

"How fortunate the three of you are," he said, "to have found such a loving home with Miss Horner. I believe a bright future awaits each of you here. 'Seek and ye shall find,' I like to say. Providence always takes care of its own." He then commented on the fine library my aunt had in the parlor, how nicely we kept the house, and of course, how much he enjoyed and appreciated the tea and delicious biscuits. I told him how much I loved to read.

"I have read almost all of these books", I confided. "Little Women and Jane Eyre are my favorites, but I like almost any book that has a good story."

After that first visit, it seemed he came to call quite often. Aunt Rebecca began to pay extra attention to her appearance and even made herself a lovely new dress for Sunday services and dinner at her home afterward. Her cheeks flushed with pleasure whenever she saw the pastor on her excursions into town. I often heard her humming and sometimes even singing softly as she worked at her dressmaking or out in the garden. My aunt's cheeks grew pink, and she would get nervous whenever the pastor came to the house (though she denied it) and we began to tease her about being sweet on Pastor Stevens. She would brush us off.

"Don't be silly" she would say, or "Heavens, how did you get such an idea? I am almost old enough to be his mother!"

Sometimes when Pastor Stevens came to see us,

he would bring a book for Lydia and me to borrow since I had told him on several occasions how much I loved to read. Soon he was enjoying dinner with us almost every week and after dinner, Pastor Stevens and my aunt strolled around the gardens for a while, talking. We would peek out the windows to see what they were doing, and giggle.

I began to hear whispers around the village that Aunt Rebecca and Pastor Stevens were "keeping company" and one late autumn day, my aunt told me that she felt sure Pastor Steven would propose to her soon. "Oh!" she said, "He is such a dear man! I know a pastor's wife has many duties, but he is proud of my talents as a dressmaker, and I feel sure he would not want me to give that up if we were to marry." My aunt was starry-eyed as she said this and I hoped, fervently, that this would be true. Sewing and creating beautiful clothing was as necessary as breathing to Aunt Rebecca. No matter how she might feel about Pastor Stevens, I felt certain she would fade away and die if she could not continue her work.

All that changed one terrible day in late fall. It was a cold and drizzly day, but inside, the fire in both our parlor and dining room fireplaces made the rooms cozy and pleasant. We were sitting at table enjoying a delicious roast of pork and spirited conversation after the morning church services when there was a loud knock at the front door. Rose jumped up to answer and soon reappeared with a young woman dressed in an old shawl over her soiled dress. The shawl had given her no protection from the heavy rain and cold and she was soaked to the skin. She was pulling an equally bedraggled looking child by the hand, a very thin little girl of perhaps seven or eight.

"This woman says she is looking for the pastor and needs his help," Rose announced. "She said she has been looking for him for a long time." In that same instance, Pastor Stevens stood up so quickly his chair toppled over backward with a crash and his face went white. It was as if he had just seen someone resurrected from the dead. Everyone at the table looked from the woman to the pastor and back again, not sure what to do until Aunt Rebecca spoke up.

"Goodness, my dears, you are both soaked through. Come here in front of the fire to warm yourselves. You must be hungry from your travels. Rose will fix a plate for each of you." The woman came to stand with the child in front of the fire, as instructed, but her gaze never left the Pastor's face.

"Hello, Gideon," she said, "or should I say, Pastor Stevens? You remember me, don't you?" There was a sneer in her voice.

I was amazed to see the pastor appear completely unnerved by this unexpected interruption.

"Nell," he said, "Of course I remember." His voice was unsteady, and he was trying to smile, but it came off crooked. "Let us go into the parlor so we can talk privately and not disturb these good people at their Sunday dinner."

"To be sure," she said, with a bite in her tone. "You would not want these fine citizens to know who you really are!" Then, turning to the little girl, who had stood woodenly by her side all this time, "Gideon, I would like to introduce you to your daughter."

There was an audible gasp from around the table.

"Please, Nell," he begged, "let us talk about this in private." Then he turned to Aunt Rebecca, and said, in a pinched voice, "I am so sorry, madam, to have troubled you with this interruption. Let us talk another time and I will explain all."

"No need to explain," my Aunt said, struggling to keep her voice steady. "We will not speak of this again. You are no longer welcome in my home. Please go and take your family with you."

"Please, Rebecca—I beg you not to do this! I love you!" However, Aunt Rebecca had already turned her back and left the room.

"Ha!" Nell said. "Serves you right!"

His face now crimson, Pastor Stevens left the table as gracefully as he was able and went out of the room with Nell and the little girl. The last I saw of them they were walking toward town with the rain and wind catching at their clothes. I heard angry words but could not make them out.

For days after that meeting, I felt as if some evil force had sucked all the joy out of our house. I often heard my Aunt sobbing behind the door to her bedroom, and when she did appear, she looked pale and haggard, no longer caring how she looked or dressed. She stopped going to church until she heard that Pastor Stevens had left town, to the great chagrin of the townsfolk, for he was much loved by everyone. I, too, missed him terribly and my heart broke for my dear aunt. I wished that somehow, we could all go back to the way things were before, but, of course, that could never be. None of us ever spoke of the pastor again.

CARY FLANAGAN

Chapter Eleven

Thank goodness for the support and comfort of friends! Aunt Rebecca was the mainstay of a quilting group that she had been hosting in our house every month for years. It was a wonderful experience for me as I was growing up, and after the fiasco with Pastor Stevens, I think the members of the group helped my aunt regain her balance through their steady presence and friendship.

Every fourth Wednesday of the month, this group would gather to quilt on a big frame in Aunt Rebecca's parlor. Ropes held the frame against the ceiling when it was not in use. It could be lowered and ready to load the next quilt in just a few minutes. I thought it a very clever arrangement. Aunt Rebecca called the group a quilting bee.

After Pastor Stevens left town, the rumors flew around as to what might have caused him to leave so suddenly. Each of my aunt's quilting friends kept silent on the subject. I think she appreciated their discretion and took comfort from it. Sometimes, one or another of the women asked me in private if I knew what had happened, but it was not my place to tell them.

I enjoyed these gatherings very much. The bee meetings were one of the few times (besides church) that we socialized with other women of the community. They provided an opportunity for simple things such as exchanging recipes, quilt block designs or sharing gossip. More importantly, they provided a comfortable place for members to express their private thoughts and feelings, something they could not do at home. For example, when Mrs. Maynard's husband took sick, and she was so worried about how she would manage if he died. (He did regain his health, but it was a long struggle).

Another time when Mrs. Jessup's baby daughter caught a fever and died. She was beside herself with grief, but the group helped her through the worst of it. Sometimes a member complained about a child who was hard to handle and asked for some advice from those who had been through this with their own children.

Conversations at our meetings ranged from entertaining to serious by turns and I took everything in as a quiet observer until I was old enough to join in.

During the years of the terrible war, many of the quilts made by this little group of compassionate women (and by other women in the village, I learned later), were sent to the men who were away fighting, and sometimes for those who returned to convalesce from their wounds. The women also rolled bandages and knit woolen socks and caps for the soldiers during those years. I was still young at the time but helped by making bundles of the socks and bandages so they would be ready to ship out.

Every month members of the bee took a turn bringing a quilt top that the group would load with backing and batting onto the frame. For most of the day and sometimes into the evening, they sat around the frame putting tiny, even stitches through all the layers of the quilt in beautiful patterns while they chatted and caught up with each other's family news.

While Lydia and I were still young, my aunt only allowed us to observe and to help serve tea and biscuits or some other treat when everyone stopped to take a rest. As we grew older and more skilled, we joined the circle and worked on a small area of the quilt in which we practiced the tiny stitches that were required. My aunt told us that occasionally one of the women picked out our stitches after we left to do our chores if they did not meet her high standards. This happened less and less often, however, as each of us gained experience.

Seven women came regularly to work on the quilts as well as one or two who came when they could. There was Aunt Rebecca, (of course), Mrs. Martha Benson (Aaron's mother), Miss Lucy Hastings, (my teacher at school) and Mrs. Helen Maynard whose husband was a shoemaker. Mrs. Polly Jessup, the doctor's wife, came every month unless her husband needed her that day in his surgery. Miss Phoebe Mason and Miss Ada Young were not yet married and lived with their parents. Mrs. Hattie Fifield joined the group when I was about twelve. Her husband made wooden furniture and barrels in a workshop nearby.

I felt funny about having Miss Hastings in the group but also pleased, in a way. I felt "special," being able to get to know her outside of the classroom. Lydia felt the same way. Miss Hastings clearly made an effort not to appear to be playing favorites when we were in school, but I could see she had become especially fond of Lydia and Lydia of her.

Mrs. Benson brought her youngest child, little Lizzy, with her to our quilting gatherings, and one of my jobs, before I was old enough to join the group, was to take care of and entertain the baby when she was not sleeping. Mrs. Benson often brought jars of cider for all of us to enjoy. The other members took turns bringing biscuits or sweets and my aunt served tea.

Everyone who participated seemed to enjoy the company and the opportunity to gossip. There were always stories circulating about the various events in town. Some of the stories really surprised me and occasionally even shocked me a little, but I always kept my eyes and ears open, and my mouth shut unless someone spoke to me directly.

If there was no new gossip to talk about at a bee meeting, the ladies took turns talking about how they and their families came to this town and when, or what the history of their property might be, and those proved to be interesting topics for discussion.

For example, I learned that Miss Hastings was an only child who had grown up in Watertown, Massachusetts, near Boston. Her grandfather had been a schoolteacher and her father a professor of history at Harvard College. Her mother had been a seamstress who taught her how to sew. She had died in childbirth along with her baby when Miss Hastings was about nine. Her father never remarried.

"I guess teaching is in my blood," she laughed. Miss Hastings (I could not call her by her given name, Lucy while I was still a pupil in her school), said she had been lonely growing up without sisters and brothers. "I think that is one of the reasons I enjoy teaching so much," she said. "I like being surrounded by lots of boys and girls and it is interesting to me to watch them learn and grow up in my classroom. Of course, some of my students are unruly and difficult," she said with a broad wink aimed at Lydia and me. I flushed. Lydia looked embarrassed but clearly enjoyed the attention.

Miss Hastings told us about Bradford Academy, the place where she had gone to boarding school to be a teacher and told us funny stories about when she was a student there. The one that sticks most in my mind is how all the girls had to sleep three in a single bed, partly because there were not enough beds but also because the dormitory had no heat, and it was the only way to stay warm at night!

After she graduated from normal school, Miss Hastings said she saw the ad for teaching in our village school.

"It was a wonderful opportunity for me," she said, "and I have been happy here," She said she did not mind renting two small rooms from Mrs. Green who ran a boarding house on the east side of town. "I don't need much—my real home is my classroom."

Another time, Mrs. Jessup, the doctor's wife, said her grandparents had moved to our village in the early 1800s when there was only a handful of farms in the area. "They moved here from over in Maine, in search of good farmland. My grandfather built the house up on Blueberry Hill where I grew up. After Grandpa died, my parents took over the farm. Dr. Jessup and I lived there for a few years after we married until our house and the doctor's office were built."

"How did you meet Dr. Jessup—I heard he came here from Boston?" asked Mrs. Benson.

"My father took me on a trip to Boston to sell off our crop of potatoes and barley when I was about eighteen. I met Dr. Jessup at the inn where we were staying. I guess I just dazzled him with my beauty and charms," she said, laughing. "He decided he wanted to follow me here and set up a new practice." It was an excellent opportunity for a young doctor, being the only doctor in the area.

"Naturally, I insisted he had to marry me!" She laughed again. "And then along came eight children, one right after the other," she said, with a mixture of pride and exasperation. "Do you know that the days I join with you ladies for our bee meetings is the only time I can have a moment to myself and to talk with like-minded adults!" She chuckled. "I am not sure I could retain my sanity without all of you!"

Miss Phoebe Mason and Miss Ada Young were the only unmarried women in the group (besides, of course, Lydia and me). Phoebe was about eighteen and had blond ringlets framing her pretty face. She reminded us often that young Samuel Walker, a nephew of Mrs. Benson's, was courting her. She was giggly and blushed a lot when she spoke of him. She said she wanted to be part of our bee so she could get quilts completed for her hope chest. Her parents, with whom she lived on a small farm a few miles from town, did not want them to marry for at least two more years. "I don't know how I will ever be able to stand waiting that long!" she said, in her high, giggling voice. There were winks around the circle and she blushed.

Miss Ada was a bit older and the opposite of Miss Phoebe. At nearly 23, town folk considered her an old maid. She appeared to feel the lack of someone in her life that she could claim as a suitor and talk about as others in the bee spoke of husbands, children, or a beau. She was tall and thin and had very dark hair pulled severely into a bun at the back of her head. I could not help wondering if she might not attract a suitor more easily if she relaxed her appearance a little and smiled more often.

Although generally quiet, I could tell Miss Ada listened closely to everything we discussed. Her father operated a gristmill to grind the wheat, corn, and barley brought to him by farmers in the surrounding area. She was an accomplished needlewoman (as was her mother, she once confided) and I was able to learn much from her by observing as she worked on a quilt.

Mrs. Maynard was a pleasant woman with ample girth and a happy disposition. Most of her children had families of their own now. With only one boy left at home, she said she was enjoying more time to sew and make quilts though there was still plenty to do with milking and feeding several cows and raising chickens, never mind taking care of the garden. Her son helped his father in the shoemaking trade when he was not in school so most of the work at home fell to her.

Mr. Maynard traveled from farm to farm and town to town measuring people's feet for shoes or boots. He expected families that raised cattle to supply their own leather. He had only a limited supply of cured leather to sell. He kept a small cobbler shop in town, where he was teaching his son how to make and repair shoes.

Mrs. Fifield was a young woman of about twenty-five. I liked her immediately when we first met. She told us she and her husband had moved here from the village of Sandwich when they were first married, a few years back. Her husband, Lucas, built beautiful furniture and they had set up a workshop near the center of town. She helped her husband by making baskets of all sizes. I was interested to discover that she also made braided rugs from scrap wool that she sold along with the furniture and baskets. They lived above their workshop and showroom and sawdust always covered everything. "I can't wait for us to be able to live in a real house with no sawdust!" she told us, laughing. Then she blushed and patted her belly. "Sawdust is no good for a baby!"

I loved hearing these stories and learning more about the women in the bee and their families. My favorite story came from Mrs. Benson. She was a friendly and "comfortable" woman. I felt drawn to her from the moment we first met in the group when I was five or six. She was a big woman with eyes that crinkled when she smiled, which was often, and she had a hearty laugh. I think she liked me from the first as well and wanted me to succeed as a quilter. She was one of the most skilled in the group, and often took extra time to help me with my stitches. I was grateful for her help and attention.

The story she told one day about the Benson Farm
and how it came to be, was the most interesting story I
heard in that group.

"My husband's grandfather, Ezra Benson, came
from Newburyport, Massachusetts in the late 1770s,"
she told us. "He wanted a large parcel of land to
develop an apple orchard and he chose a 500-acre
parcel, sight unseen, by looking at a map. He paid
twenty-five pounds for it, a large sum in those days.
We still have the bill of sale in a frame on the wall of
my husband's office. No roads existed in the area at
that time and there were no other settlements except
Tamworth and Sandwich to the west.

"With only a compass to guide him, he traversed
Indian trails northward through the forest until he
found the coordinates for his parcel. Mind you, he was
only a young man of twenty when he first came here.
He spent several summers clearing the land alone with
only an ax and saw, walking home to Newburyport
in late fall each year. In the fourth summer, he built a
three-room cabin and in the fifth summer, he brought
his brother, Daniel, with him and they started building
the large, center-chimney colonial house you still
see on our hill. They milled all the floorboards and
wainscoting planks from the trees on Ezra's land. Some
of the boards were more than 24 inches wide!

"The two brothers eventually found themselves
brides in a nearby settlement—two sisters, as luck
would have it. Ezra and his new wife, Molly finished
clearing the land and planted hundreds of apple tree
saplings. Daniel and his bride settled nearby and began

clearing land for raising sheep, but eventually moved back to Newburyport. Apparently, it was too rough a life for them.

"One early winter morning after the house was finished, Ezra and Molly woke up to find several Indians asleep on the hearth in front of the fire in the kitchen. After all, the house stood on an old Indian trail, so I guess they felt entitled! Molly gave them hot coffee and bread and they went on their way."

Shocked murmurs passed around the quilt frame.

Mrs. Benson continued, "It plumb makes me tired thinking about all the two of them did to make that farm work. However, it paid off in the end—they eventually shipped apples to Europe as well as all over the east coast." In the next generation, she said, they added two huge barns and raised a hundred head of dairy cows in addition to growing apples and eventually they added sheep and pigs. It became one of the most successful farms in the area. "

"After more than a century, the farm still bears the Benson name," Mrs. Benson concluded with great pride.

One of the things I loved best about participating in the monthly bee meetings was seeing the different quilt patterns that our friends and neighbors made and their color choices. We often shared patterns for blocks and ideas for how to lay them out into a finished design. We also traded fabric scraps, since it was not always easy to purchase the fabric needed for a particular quilt.

Sometimes Miss Ada or Mrs. Benson, the two most accomplished appliquéers among us, designed and sewed a vine covered with pretty flowers to weave around the outside border of a quilt or garlands gracefully curving around the inside edge of a quilt to form a frame. A quilt might also have bouquets of flowers or some other applique design alternating with pieced blocks.

I learned so many new techniques and discovered so many new ways to design and construct a quilt I sometimes thought my brain would burst! All this new information kept me excited and energized until it was time for our next meeting.

CARY FLANAGAN

Chapter Twelve

Journal Entry, October 1870

Dearest Mama - A truly remarkable thing has happened. You would never believe it. A few months ago, a railroad company out of Boston laid tracks right through the center of the village. I could hear the men working all the way from Aunt Rebecca's house. The tracks run up the west side of the lake from the south and continue north right into the mountains. They also built a station house next to the tracks. I can see it from my bedroom window. There was much celebration and merriment in the village when the first trains arrived in town. I enjoy walking down to the station with my friends to see them pull into the station. It is so much fun to see what these strangers from far away look like. I am amazed at all the fancy clothes and the many trunks and servants brought by the rich people who come to visit for the summer. Some of them even bring their little lap dogs! The fresh mountain air and beautiful clear lakes draw them here. Some of them come from as far away as New York! It makes me wonder, sometimes, what life might be like where these people come from. Do you think I will ever be able to travel and to see more of the world than just what is here? I want to learn, explore and discover new things! Some people are saying the trains will change everything in our little village but I, for one, think it will be a good thing. I wish you could be here to see these things for yourself, Mama.

Your loving daughter, Hannah

·ം൭ൈൟ·

I finished my very first quilt the same year the railway arrived. I was twelve. I was eager to be as good a quilter as the women in our bee, and I was thrilled when I completed the quilt top and my bee friends placed it on the big frame for quilting. It was only simple squares interspersed with four-patch blocks, but I was so excited and pleased with myself, I could hardly stand it! It was an exhilarating experience to see my simple quilt top transformed into a beautiful quilt, stitch by stitch, before my very eyes! I received many compliments from the women, and Aunt Rebecca told me when it was finished how proud she was of me. She suggested I place the quilt in my hope chest after I had finished sewing on the binding, but I wanted to put it right on my bed where I could see it every day. I knew then that I had found my "calling."

After that, I worked in earnest to learn how to make some of the complex blocks that the other quilters in our bee made for their quilts. Often there were no patterns and if there was no existing block design to copy, the women sketched out drawings of the blocks they wanted to make and then made paper templates. They showed me how to cut out different sections of a block and sew them together by hand. My first attempts at fancy blocks were pitiful but I gradually got better at it and soon learned how to sew the pieces together on Aunt Rebecca's treadle machine.

When I was thirteen, I had made enough blocks for another quilt, this one larger and more beautiful than my first. It was in shades of blue set off with white, my favorite color combination, and I used a block called Birds in the Air. I was excited to have it quilted by our friends in the bee and when they finished, I put it on my bed and felt quite pleased with myself!

I decided to set a goal for myself to complete one twelve-inch block that was new to me each month. After I made enough for a large quilt, I could put all the blocks together as a sampler with sashing in between them. There would need to be thirty blocks all together to make the quilt as large as I wanted it to be—a daunting task.

I decided to make each block in whatever colors were available to me and not worry about whether the colors matched. I wanted to do something different from the other quilts I saw. Whenever I had some time to myself, I worked on the block designs. I picked the fabrics from Aunt Rebecca's scrap bag, and at the end of every month, I completed at least one twelve-inch block. I always looked forward to bringing my new blocks to the sewing bee and hearing the comments and suggestions that the other women made.

Soon after my fourteenth birthday, I completed enough blocks that I thought were good enough for my new quilt and worked hard to sew them all together. I found a blue fabric that I liked for sashing strips between the blocks and around the outside that helped make the quilt design look more unified. I was thrilled when Aunt Rebecca told me I could purchase enough fabric to make a wide border and maybe even enough for the back of the quilt. Just think—we could go to the general store and spend money for new fabric! Aunt Rebecca told me it would be her gift to me after working so hard and so long on this special quilt. I almost cried!

I still remember the afternoon we went to the general store to pick out a pretty fabric for my quilt. I took the quilt top with me and was so proud showing it off to Jane and her mother. Mrs. McNally and my aunt helped me choose a flowered cotton that had a lot of the same blue in it as the sashing. It seemed almost magical to me that we could find such a perfect fabric for the quilt borders. We were also able to buy enough of a lighter blue cotton for the back. We had to get more thread too! I skipped home I was so delighted.

...

Journal Entry, September 1873

Dearest Mama – I know I do not write often enough but I think of you every day. A truly wonderful thing has happened. Aunt R's horse, Jewel, has given birth to a beautiful brown filly. Aunt R. said I could keep her and raise her myself. I am so excited but also a bit scared. That is a big responsibility! There is a hired man named Henry Blackwell who has been taking care of Jewel and the other animals for some years for Aunt Rebecca. He will teach me what I need to know. When the time came for the birth, Mr. Blackwell asked me if I wanted to be there. Of course, I did! It was quite an experience. I did not like to see Jewel in pain, but Mr. Blackwell said the mare had given birth several times already and she knew just what to do.

My first job was to help clean the blood and mess off the tiny foal and I was surprised at how quickly she was able to get on her feet and find her mother's milk. I will feed her and help keep her stall clean once she no longer needs her mother. I have decided to name her Molly. I think we will become good friends. I have had another interesting experience recently. I found a copy of Uncle Tom's Cabin by Harriet Beecher Stowe in Aunt Rebecca's library, and I read the entire heartbreaking story. Now I have a much better understanding of the War Between the States and the Cause for which my father died. I am anxious to see when and how the terrible wounds left by the war will heal. I am happy that slavery and the unbearable suffering of so many people has finally ended, but I suspect it may be a long time before white people and black people, especially in the South, will be able to live alongside each other as equals.

Your loving daughter, Hannah

⁓

Chapter Thirteen

1873

Soon after school started in the fall, a man came to our school with two little girls and a boy. He spoke no English, only French, but Miss Hastings knew a little French and she understood that he and several other families had come down from Canada looking for work. He said he wanted his children to learn English while he was away seeking employment and a place for their group to settle. He said he would be unable to pay right away but that he did not want charity. He promised to pay as soon as he could. Apparently, his wife had found a local farm family to stay with temporarily. Miss Hastings agreed, as long as someone brought the children every morning and fetched them home again in the afternoon.

The youngest girl was only five, too young for school, but I offered to help her learn our language if she was willing. Her name was Aimee. She was a sweet little girl, blonde like me, with blue eyes and a big smile that lit up her face. Her sister, Marie-Claire, was about nine and had long wavy brown hair and solemn eyes. Francois was almost twelve and very thin. He was tall for his age and had a sullen look as if he had come to school against his will. Marie-Claire just stood quietly and seemed to take everything in.

Miss Hastings asked Jane to work with Marie-Claire and Aaron to help Francois, and it was not long before all three children became comfortable in our little school and began, haltingly at first but then with more confidence, to learn English. I loved working with Aimee. She was a joy, laughing easily when she made mistakes. It was as if learning a new language was a game for her and she picked it up quickly. I taught her to sound out the letters and to read out of a simple primer and she was pleased with herself when she was able to get through it without stumbling over every word.

Marie-Claire also picked up the language quite easily and moved on to some of the regular classroom studies. Francois kept himself on guard but gradually began to relax. Aaron was very patient with him and I could see that they were becoming friends. He, too, began to pick up our language, but it was a struggle for him.

Two months after their arrival, their father came to pay Miss Hastings and announced that his family, along with the others, were moving further north where there was plentiful work cutting lumber from the heavily forested mountains. He said there was a small school for the children of the lumbermen who worked in that area. I was happy that the children would be able to continue their studies, but I was sorry to see them leave.

I had hoped that they would stay and that we

could continue to be friends. Aimee was close to tears when their father came for them for the last time. "Will I ever see you again?" she asked me, sniffling. "Maybe you can come and visit me some day?" she said hopefully.

"I would like that very much," I told her. She gave me a big hug and then she was gone.

Journal Entry, November 1873

Dearest Mama – I miss the little Canadian girl, Aimee, very much. She and her sister and brother left a few days ago to go north with their parents. It is so hard to make a friend and then have to say goodbye. I feel like a part of me has gone with her. I hope I can visit her when I get older. Why is it that people have to go away? Sometimes I feel so empty, as if I have a large hole inside of me that I cannot fill, or as if I am missing a part of who I am. I do not know what to do when I feel this way. I am very sad today and missing you.

Your hurting daughter, Hannah

Journal Entry, late November 1873

Dearest Mama — It is strange how you can feel sad one day and then happy again the next. Sometimes I feel all mixed up. I wish so much I could talk to you. Often, I feel sad and do not know why but my friends can always make me laugh and can bring me back to feeling happy again. I am so grateful to have them in my life.

Do you remember me telling you about a boy at school named Aaron, the one who used to help me with my math and who helped the young French-Canadian boy learn English? He walked Lydia, Rose, and me home from school today. Aunt R. made us hot chocolate because it was a chilly and raw day and he stayed to visit for a while.

I really like him, Mama. He is one of my closest friends. He is so easy to talk to—not like the other boys who only want to tease and poke fun at the girls. Lydia says she thinks he likes me too. I get a funny feeling inside sometimes when he looks at me. He is sixteen now and beginning to look quite grown up. He has dark curly hair and dark fuzz just starting to show on his face and his voice sometimes cracks and is getting deeper. It is funny when that happens, but he gets self-conscious about it. I find it endearing. He is also remarkably strong from all the farm work he does, and he is becoming quite handsome. The best thing about him, Mama, is that he is not shy at all. He always has a smile ready and loves to talk. He is really helping me to become more confident around other people.

How does a girl know when she is in love, Mama? When did you know? I have been thinking about this a lot lately. I wish I had someone I could talk to about it. After what happened with Pastor Stevens, I cannot ask Aunt Rebecca. I wonder if I could ask Jane's mother or even Mrs. Benson.

Your loving daughter, Hannah

.⁓⤸⁓.

Chapter Fourteen

By the time I was sixteen and Aaron seventeen, he was my constant companion. Other children began to tease us: "Who is Hannah sweet on?" "When are you going to pop the question, Aaron?" We just laughed and ignored them. Sometimes I felt as if I was not spending enough time with Lydia and Jane, but they both liked Aaron and I think they understood. Sometimes, the four of us would get involved with some activity together, and Aaron would ask one of his brothers to join us, but bit-by-bit, Aaron and I spent almost all our time just the two of us when we were not in school or needed elsewhere. We had to be careful since we had reached an age when it was not seemly for us to spend time alone together. Fortunately, Aunt Rebecca and Aaron's parents pretended not to notice, for which we were grateful. Neither of us spoke of the change.

Aaron's father, William Benson, owned a large farm northwest of the village, the one that Mrs. Benson told us about at the quilting bee. The first time I saw it, I was overwhelmed. It was an imposing white farmhouse with black shutters framing the windows and an enormous red barn just below the crest of a hill. If you looked out over the cleared fields from the veranda, you could see across the rolling hills to the south and the shimmering lake and village in the distance.

To the north, down the back of their hill, the forest was thick with great pines and hemlocks. Another small lake glimmered here and there through the trees. A long path meandered from behind the barn, through the forest, all the way down to the shore of this lake. Beyond that, mountains rose in overlapping waves until they were lost in a blue haze.

Sheep and cows grazed in the fields near the top of the hill and a large apple orchard planted by Aaron's great grandparents spread out below the house. Two of Aaron's brothers, Will, and Jesse had already completed school and helped their father run the farm. His brother, Daniel, was almost finished and eager to join his brothers.

After church on Sundays, Aaron and I walked together through the Benson orchard or down the path behind the barn to the water. I loved the smell of the pines and the ground was heavy with their needles so that the walking was easy underfoot. The path ended in a little cove and I could see only a small part of the lake but what I could see was beautiful and serene. The walk back up that hill was a challenge, though!

Our favorite time of year was spring when the apple trees were in full bloom. Oh, you have never seen such a sight! Standing at the top of the orchard, all you could see was a sea of pink and white blossoms below.

When we could, we sneaked away with a picnic basket and a quilt to spend an afternoon in a secluded portion of the orchard. The smell of the blossoms was intoxicating. We talked for hours and held hands. On a particularly beautiful day, which I will never forget, Aaron shyly asked me if he could kiss me. I said yes! It was a lovely first kiss, the first of many, stolen in the rare moments when we could be completely alone.

In the fall, I joined Aaron, his family, some neighbors, and hired hands picking the apples, dozens of bushels full of different varieties and colors. We had to sort the apples and prepare them for shipping. Then came the cider making with the drops and lower quality apples. Aaron's mother and I prepared the large gallon bottles while the men filled the wooden cider press with apples. Aaron's little sister, Lizzy, who was almost six, begged to be allowed to help. We kept her busy picking up stray apples and taking them over to her brothers who were taking turns turning the heavy handle of the press. The press squashed the apples to a pulp, squeezing out the juice, which ran into a large bucket. The pigs behind the barn enjoyed eating the leftover pulp, or "mash". What a treat for them! You could hear their squeals of delight when they received a fresh supply.

Oh, the bees and wasps that flew around us, attracted by such sweetness! How I loved the first taste of the fresh cider, which I sneaked as Mrs. Benson and I filled the bottles with the golden liquid. Afterward, exhausted and covered in sticky juice, we sat on the front veranda of the Benson's large farmhouse while we enjoyed glasses of sweet cider and homemade donuts in the glow of the setting sun. At the end of the day, everyone went home with several gallons of cider and aching backs.

Mrs. Benson and I developed a warm and friendly relationship. She told me how much she appreciated my help during the apple picking and cider making and the loaves of fresh bread and jam I brought along to share. Although she never said anything, I think she was happy to see the friendship between Aaron and me blossoming. I also enjoyed getting to know Mr. Benson and Aaron's older brothers in such an informal setting. This family was very close-knit and affectionate with each other. I felt fortunate to be able to spend time with them though I was also a little bit jealous of the bonds and camaraderie they shared. Much as I loved my Aunt Rebecca, Lydia, and Rose, I longed for a complete family of my own.

Gradually, as Aaron and I grew older, our affection for each other deepened into something more and there came a time when I knew, in my heart, that Aaron would always be a part of my life, and that his family would be my family.

Journal Entry, March 1874

Dearest Mama, the long winter is finally ending. Warm days and freezing nights have made conditions just right for maple sugaring this year — some say it is the best it has been in many years. There are sugar maples all over town and you can see buckets hanging on them everywhere. Several farmers have gotten together to pool their efforts and share the syrup or profits later. They built a large sugarhouse on the main road a mile or so east of the village center, where it will be easy for the men gathering sap to empty the heavy buckets into the metal evaporation pans. Aaron and I asked if we could help, as the Bensons were tapping several maples on their land but not enough to have their own sugarhouse. This past week, Jesse and Will brought wagonloads of sap down to the village every morning, and Aaron and I helped with the evaporation process all day inside the sugar house and kept the fire going in the big oven. The work is hard and it sure is hot and steamy in there! However, the rewards at the end of the day are worth it — bottles of syrup to take home and a special treat of sugar on snow, my favorite sweet. It is astonishing how many gallons of sap you need to boil down to get a small bottle of syrup! I had no idea before helping with the sugaring this week.

Oh, Mama! I am in love! I am sure in my heart now that Aaron is The One! He has not spoken for me yet, but I do not think it will be long. I feel giddy thinking about it. Can you believe — I have reached the age that you were when you married! I think Aaron and I are too young yet. It is best we wait a while longer — but waiting is so hard!

Your loving daughter, Hannah

Chapter Fifteen

In the spring of 1875, a black family arrived in town and asked if they could stay for a few days. They were apparently looking for a place to settle after a long journey all the way from Georgia. I soon learned that they had been slaves on a big plantation and became free when Sherman's army swept through the South, destroying everything in its path—plantations, entire towns—and taking whatever food, horses, and livestock they found to feed the army. Hundreds of black folks had followed the Union soldiers, not knowing where else to go. It was a difficult and desperate time, even while the emancipated slaves rejoiced in their freedom.

This family consisted of an older man, perhaps in his sixties, and a younger couple with three young children, two boys and a little girl. The family had not brought much with them except a mule pulling a dilapidated wagon containing a few household items and tools. They only brought what they and the mule could carry when they left the plantation—a few personal possessions and some of the elder man's blacksmithing tools. Fortunately, they had earned enough money along the way to buy food and were able to purchase the old wagon by taking odd jobs and working in smithies as they made their way north.

Naturally, these folks were a great curiosity in our village. No one I knew had ever seen a black person, except perhaps a few of the men who had fought in the war and were lucky enough to return home or individuals who had been to Boston or other larger cities on business. Some people welcomed them and offered assistance in finding shelter and food. However, there was grumbling among other residents who apparently thought the family should keep moving further north.

The family kept mostly to themselves, at first, until they knew if they were staying or would have to try somewhere else. Mrs. Green, who ran the boarding house east of town, offered to let them stay there until they could work out a more permanent arrangement. Unlike some of our neighbors, my friends and I thought their arrival in town a most interesting turn of events and we were very curious to find out more about them.

After school, the next day, Aaron, Lydia, Jane, and I decided we wanted to meet the newcomers. I was impressed that they had worked so hard and had persevered through such difficult circumstances to make their way here. The least we could do was introduce ourselves and offer some words of welcome and encouragement. Lydia and I made several loaves of bread, Jane brought a wedge of cheese from the general store, and Aaron brought a gallon of cider. We went together in Aunt Rebecca's wagon to Mrs. Green's boarding house. The mother introduced herself.

"My name is Clara," she said. "This here be George," she said, gesturing to the tallest of the three children. "This is Billy and the little one is Sallie Mae."

George stared at us solemnly, but the young ones only peeked out from behind their mother's skirt. We introduced ourselves in turn and offered the food to Clara. George's eyes grew big when he saw what we brought, and he grinned.

The four of them looked exhausted from their travels—Clara said they had been on the road for several days, coming up through Massachusetts from Connecticut. She was very thin – it did not look as if she or her children had eaten recently. However, she was courteous and friendly and appreciated the food and cider that we brought. The younger children hid behind her the whole time we were there. Clara said the two men were in the next room, sleeping.

"What made you decide to come here?" I asked Clara.

"We heard that the folks in New Hampshire is more accepting of folks like us," she said. "We thought we best keep going north. A man told us there be a blacksmith in this town and maybe he needs some extra help."

Clara's way of speaking was so foreign to me it was sometimes difficult to make out what she was saying, but I pieced together some of her story. The family's last name was Foster—the name of the owner of the plantation where they had been slaves. Clara told us that the older man, Amos, had been a blacksmith on the plantation and his son, John, trained as a farrier, shoeing all the horses and mules on the plantation. The two of them worked together in the plantation smithy instead of in the fields, for which they were grateful. John and Clara lived together as husband and wife but were not legally married. Their former owner did not allow marriage between slaves and they were afraid to marry on the way north in case someone traced their names. Even though the war was over, and they were free, they were still afraid someone might send them back to Georgia. After reading Uncle Tom's Cabin, I could certainly understand their fear.

"I been a house slave," Clara said, "up at the Big House. I was learned how to cook and do the laundry for Massa's family. Missus be kind to me, but not old Massa." She looked away with a grimace. Clara had light skin, almost white, which I wondered about since I had seen her husband and he was very dark. However, I was too polite to ask. It looked as if she was expecting another child. I was full of curiosity but did not want to pry.

George had been born shortly before the war ended and was an infant when they fled north. He was skinny as a rail now but had a big smile that lit up his dark face. The younger two children, Billy, and Sallie Mae had been born along the way. They, too, were very thin and seemed small for their ages (six and four). They were the color of coffee with cream in it.

On our way home, Lydia and I decided to ask the members of our bee to help us provide this family with food until they were able to earn their keep. We also agreed to ask Miss Hastings about allowing the two older children to attend school. No one in the family could read or write except what little they had been able to pick up on the way north. I thought that perhaps Miss Hastings or a group of us girls could tutor them. We were full of grand ideas and plans!

A few days later, Lydia and I visited Clara and the children again at the boarding house, bringing more bread, cheese, and fresh goat's milk for the children. Amos and John were out looking for work. Clara told us they had spoken with the only blacksmith in town, a Mr. Jackson, to see if he needed extra help. Mr. Jackson had told them they could work a few hours a week to start and then they could talk about a more permanent arrangement after he saw what kind of work they could do. I had never met Mr. Jackson myself but had heard he was an honest man. He was also getting on in years. I was hopeful something good would come of this possibility.

There was only one bed in the room. A quilt lay over the bed unlike any I had ever seen before. Very bright colors, especially yellows and reds accented the squares, surrounded by a lot of black fabric. The design was a series of picture stories like an album quilt or sampler. The maker had cut every figure carefully, whether a person, animal, tree or whatever it might be, out of many different fabrics and appliquéd them with tiny stitches to the muslin background.

"Clara," I said, "this quilt is beautiful and so unusual. I have never seen one like it. Did you make it?"

"I have been workin' on makin' it ever since we left Georgia and it is finally finished." She beamed at my interest and compliment. "Missus taught me and two other house slaves how to sew when I was just a young-un. I have made many quilts over the years but of course, they all belonged to Massa's family. This here quilt is the very first one I made just for my own self!" I could see and feel her pride in her accomplishment.

"Tell me about these scenes in the quilt. What stories do they tell?"

"These be the story of my life, some before and some after we be freed. See here is my husband working over the blacksmith forge. And over here be the little cabin we called home."

Clara continued pointing out the various blocks. I could see the figures in the blocks depicted both black and white people along with horses and cattle—in fact, they showed many of the various activities one might see on a farm or plantation. There was a scene of slaves bent over picking cotton with heavy baskets on their backs, and another scene showed two little black boys by the side of a river, fishing with a pile of fish beside them. There was a white man sitting on a big horse holding a whip in his hand. A black woman sewing on a large quilt filled another square. In addition to scenes of slaves working, there were also birds flying and flowers in bloom, lambs, and chickens. A vine with fanciful flowers meandered around the outside edge of the quilt and the sun, in one corner, sent beams of bright light over the surface of the quilt.

"These here," Clara said pointing to the flowers, birds, and animals, "these be Freedom and Love, and the sun be the Glory of God which shines on us all and will see us through to the Promised Land."

The very last square, in the lower right corner, showed a black couple with a little baby driving a wagon pulled by a mule, heading off into the unknown.

"That last block?" Clara said with pride, "That be us on our way to a better life!"

The creativity and skill with which Clara had made this quilt touched me deeply. This wonderful quilt got me to thinking— perhaps I could invite Clara to become part of our quilting bee. I resolved to ask the group the next time we met how they would feel about that.

Journal Entry, May 1875

Dearest Mama—A most singular thing has happened. A family of former slaves has come to our town looking for a place to settle after a long and difficult journey north after the war.

They are a great curiosity as no one in these parts has ever seen anyone with dark skin and now we have a whole family! I must remind myself not to stare at them! Mrs. Green, who has rooms to let on the other side of town, has been kind enough to provide two rooms at her establishment until they can find a suitable place of their own.

I am grateful for their freedom and for the kindness of some of the citizens in our village in helping this family to feel welcome. I also know there are some who do not want them here. Time will tell how things will work out—I just hope there will not be any trouble.

Lydia and I, with Aaron's assistance, are taking food to the family. It makes me feel good to be able to help them, even if it is only a little. Miss Hastings is going to help Clara and the children learn to read and write, Amos and John too, if they want to. She lives in the same boarding house as the Fosters so it will be convenient. And Mama, you will never guess—Clara is a quilt maker!

I know some people in town are not happy about their arrival, but I think it is the most interesting thing to have happened in our village since the trains arrived. I am curious to see what happens next.

Your loving daughter, Hannah

CARY FLANAGAN

Chapter Sixteen

At our bee meeting the following month, I got up my courage to ask the group about Clara. I had already spoken with Aunt Rebecca and she thought it a fine idea, but of course, everyone would have to agree.

I waited until everyone had settled comfortably around the big frame and had started stitching on a new quilt.

"I know you have all heard about the new family of former slaves that moved into town," I said, looking around the circle to see if I could see a reaction. "I have met the family. They are nice people, friendly and eager to find work so they can support themselves. I have been getting to know Clara, the young mother, and have learned that she is a skilled quilt maker, like each of us. She showed me a quilt that she made over the many months she and her family have been making their way north. It is a true work of art. I want very much to invite her to meet all of you and to show you her quilt. And after that, I hope you might consider asking her to join our group." I paused.

"Clara is also skilled in cooking and doing

laundry and is anxious to find work. She told me her family does not wish to be a burden on anyone."

There was animated chatter around the quilt frame that went on for some time. Thankfully, everyone agreed that Clara could come to our next meeting, if she wanted to, although two members, Mrs. Maynard, and Miss Ada Young said they were not sure how they would feel having her as a regular member of the bee. However, they agreed, at least, to meet her. I was pleased.

I went in the wagon with Jewel to fetch Clara and little Sallie Mae and brought them and Clara's wonderful quilt to the next meeting. Everyone greeted them in a friendly, though guarded manner, and we made the introductions all around.

Clara appeared to be uncomfortable at first and Sallie Mae clung to her skirts and hid behind her for much of our time together. However, just as I had hoped, the women crowded around Clara's quilt and exclaimed over the fine appliqué stitches, the wonderful bright colors, and especially about the stories depicted in each block. Although the style of the quilt was wildly different from any quilt any of us had seen before, we all recognized the passion and skill with which Clara had sewn every stitch.

The following month, after the members of the bee had had a chance to talk about Clara joining the group, Aunt Rebecca invited Clara to join us, and she accepted with pleasure. By this time, her belly was large, and the members of the bee asked her shyly about when she was due. Clara flushed with embarrassment.

"October, I think. All my babies except for my oldest be born in freedom. Thank the Lord!" she said with feeling. There was a chorus of "Amen" from around the circle.

Every month after that I went with Molly and the wagon to fetch Clara and Sallie Mae to our bee meetings. It was a bit awkward at first, as everyone began to know Clara and she learned more about each member. Sadly, Mrs. Mason decided she did not want to remain in the bee. We were sorry to see her go. Miss Ada chose to stay, but told us, out of Clara's hearing, that her parents must never know that a black woman and her child were now part of the bee.

Despite these things, it did not take Clara long before she became a valued contributor in the group. Sallie Mae behaved very well and seemed eager to take in everything. She even came out from behind her mother's skirts and played quietly on the floor nearby while her mother worked on the quilt with the others.

Journal Entry, July 1875

Dearest Mama I am happy to tell you that Clara Foster has joined our quilting bee and her family seems to be settling into the community. I am so happy they will stay! Already Clara has found some paying work— several members of our bee hired her to do their laundry, so she has been able to get a small business established in town. She told me that that Mr. Jackson, the blacksmith, agreed to take on Amos and John. He injured his right arm a few weeks ago and decided it was time to retire. It is a good thing that Amos and John have found work, with six mouths to feed and another one on the way.

At our meeting this month, Clara told of her life on the plantation in Georgia and about her family's long trek north to freedom, just as the other members of the bee have told their stories of how they came to live in our village. She also told us how grateful she and her family are to have found a place of acceptance, at last.

Clara has offered to teach us how to make appliqué blocks similar to the ones in her quilt, only they will represent our own stories. I have not yet decided what "story" I want to tell in my block, but I am thinking about a "picture" of me sewing on Aunt Rebecca's beautiful sewing machine. It will be an interesting challenge!

I really like Clara. She is a strong and independent woman, and so brave to have survived all she endured as a slave. I like her little girl Sallie Mae too—she is sweet and remarkably well behaved. She brought a slate and some chalk with her to the last meeting and showed me how she is learning to write some of the letters of the alphabet. *Miss Hastings says she is a quick learner. Several of the women have offered baby clothes and blankets for the baby that is coming. I could see how touched Clara was by their kindness.*

Your loving daughter, Hannah

Journal Entry, October 1875

Dearest Mama – Clara's time came yesterday, and Aunt Rebecca and I assisted Mrs. Carter, the midwife, in the birth. After a long and difficult labor, Clara's baby finally came and it was white or very nearly, like Clara herself. It was another beautiful little girl with dark eyes and a head of very curly dark hair. Clara has decided to call her Grace. When John came to see his little girl, he marveled over her as any new father would. Then Amos and the other children came to see her. Clara was exhausted so Aunt Rebecca suggested they come back today, which they did. Baby Grace is adorable and seems to be healthy and strong.

I wish I knew how baby Grace came to be so light skinned when her Papa is so dark. It is a puzzle to me. Perhaps I will find out in time. Meanwhile, I am helping Clara with the new baby so she can rest.

Your loving daughter, Hannah

Journal Entry, May 1896

Dearest Mama — Life is so strange, sometimes. Yesterday, Jesse (Aaron's brother), asked if he could speak to me in strictest confidence. I thought, at first, he must want to speak on behalf of Aaron. I was surprised when, instead, he told me he was in love with Lydia! He told me he had tried, often, to engage her in conversation, or to invite her to go walking with him and that she had steadfastly declined, though not unkindly, every time. He did not want to give her up completely until he had proof that his love was hopeless. He begged me to speak to her on his behalf.

Oh, Mama — what a difficult position to be in! Lydia is my dearest friend!

However, today I did speak to her, and to my great surprise and chagrin, she stated very clearly, that although she likes Jesse well enough, she has decided that she does not wish to marry anyone! It is, in fact, her intention to remain unmarried for the rest of her life. I tried to ask her why, and she simply said that she is happy with her life the way it is.

I must respect her wishes but I do not understand. I do not yet know what I will say to Jesse. My heart feels sad for him. I hope he will find another love in time.

Your loving daughter, Hannah

Chapter Seventeen

1876

One day, two months before my nineteenth birthday, Aaron said he had something to show me. He said it was at some distance.

"Wear your gardening dress," he instructed. "We will be traveling part way by canoe and I do not want to soil this pretty one." That was all he would say even though I teased him to tell me more.

I packed a picnic lunch and we set out from my aunt's house early in the morning in my aunt's wagon with my horse Molly in front and a canoe and one of my old quilts and the picnic basket in the back. I still remember how curious I was but also how happy I felt just to be beside Aaron and going on what felt like an adventure together.

My aunt clucked a bit about us going off by ourselves with no chaperone but later I learned she had been in on Aaron's secret. In fact, she confided to me later, Aaron, just like the proper young man that he was, came to her to ask permission for my hand in marriage. Of course, she said yes!

We followed a dirt road out of the village for several miles until we came to a lakeshore with a little sandy beach. The lake was not as big as Easton Lake but was very pretty and lined all around with dense woods. Occasional boulders shone white along the shore or peaked from among the trees on higher ground. Beyond the trees, in the distance, I saw mountains rising to the north and west of the lake and there was a rocky cliff face to the east. To the south lay two hills that came straight down to the shore with a valley in between. The effect was of a gigantic bowl filled with water. The sun was shining brightly and there was a slight rippling breeze. I saw sparkling lights dancing off the surface of the water. It was a lovely sight. I was enchanted.

Aaron helped me get into the front seat of his small wooden canoe (no small feat with my long skirts). He showed me how to hold a paddle and how to balance my weight on the seat. Then he got into the back seat and pushed us off onto the lake. At first, I was nervous—I had never been in a canoe and did not know how to swim. The canoe tipped precariously a few times and I squeaked in fear, but soon I began to understand how to hold my body steady and move the paddle through the water without rocking the boat.

We paddled until my arms were aching, towards the valley between the two hills.

"Look, Hannah, see over there, in front of us," Aaron said. "Do you see that fallen tree in the water? That is where we are headed." We landed to the right of the dead tree and I saw a rough path rising away from the water towards a small clearing. When we reached the clearing, I saw piles of large logs with the bark removed. All around us were huge pine and hemlock trees, also spruce and the lighter green of maples and birch just beginning to leaf.

Aaron looked mightily pleased with himself. He opened his arms wide and turned around in a circle.

"What do you think, Hannah?" he said. He was grinning from ear to ear, but also seemed a bit nervous. I was not sure what Aaron expected me to say.

"The lake is very pretty," I said. "The view is beautiful—I love the clear water and the mountains. It is so quiet and peaceful here."

As I looked around the clearing, I began to understand why Aaron might have brought me there. I decided to tease him a little and pretend innocence.

"Where are we, Aaron? Why are we here?"

He blushed crimson and said, all in a rush:

"I have been hoping you might like this place, Hannah. Do you like it? I want to marry you and live my days with you here." Before I could say anything, he went on "I have great plans—a house just here, (spreading his arms), a barn over there (we will have to take out lots more trees), a big garden just beyond the house, and lots of children!" He held out his arms to me.

As I came close beside him, he whispered, "Will you marry me, Hannah? Will you take me as your husband and be my bride? Will you come and live with me here?" I answered him with a kiss and a whisper in his ear, "Yes Aaron, yes! With all my heart."

I remember his arms going around me, and my heart beating so hard I could barely breathe. My tummy was doing jumping jacks. We kissed again, deeply, and then he whispered,

"If we could marry right now in this beautiful place, would you say yes?" I was trembling as I whispered "yes." "Do you understand what I am asking of you?" I held him close and breathed "Yes."

We lay together then on our picnic quilt, our long-held passion finally unleashed, all thoughts of food forgotten. We lay entwined and were married in the eyes of God and of the birds that flew overhead and all the little forest creatures that chirped in the underbrush. At the final moment we each whispered: "I thee wed." It was the happiest moment of my life.

When Aaron brought me home that night, I felt sure Aunt Rebecca would read in my face what had happened. I blushed furiously but she was kind and only asked if I enjoyed my afternoon with Aaron. I finally blurted out "I am so happy, Aunt Rebecca! Aaron asked me to marry him, and I said yes!" "I am so happy for you both," she said, hugging me tight.

Journal Entry, June 1876

Oh, Mama—I can hardly breathe I am so happy! Aaron asked me to marry him today! Can you believe it? Mama—I am blushing as I write this—I am his and he is mine. I can still feel his hands on me, and the passion of his kisses. I feel giddy as if I could just float in the air. Is this the way you felt about Papa? Now I think I finally understand.

Your loving daughter, Hannah.

CARY FLANAGAN

Chapter Eighteen

1886-1887

Aaron told me later that the place where he took me across the lake was part of a large woodlot that his grandfather purchased long ago, almost a hundred acres. It bordered the rest of his family's land. The little cove at the bottom of the long path behind his parent's barn was on this same lake, beyond a peninsula and large island where we could not see it. Aaron had fished this pond all his life and had found this spot years ago. It had been his dream ever since then to live on this land. It was a wedding present from his parents to the two of us.

All that winter, Aaron, and his brothers cut trees around the clearing where Aaron first brought me. They went into the woods on snowshoes to fell the trees and later brought in a large sledge drawn by oxen to bring the logs to the building site. They cleaned the bark off each tree with an adze, notched the logs where they would join, then left them to season until spring.

They measured out an area for a large foundation and pounded stakes into the ground where the corners and other support posts would eventually go. Before the snow melted in early spring, they cleared more trees along a path that eventually became a road to our beautiful spot on the lake.

All the bricks for the fireplace and chimneys, as well as the granite slabs that would support the sills and corner posts arrived at the building site on a sledge pulled by a pair of oxen across the frozen lake. It took many trips to get all these materials to the building site because of the risk of overloading the sledge and having it go through the ice with the oxen!

Aaron was excited about his plans for the new house and every day he brought me updates on the progress he and his team were making. He had drawn out a rough sketch for the house, where each room would be, and asked me what I thought should go here, how big each room should be, where he should put bookcases (for, of course, there would be bookcases!). It was fun working on the plan together, trying to visualize the layout and be a part of the planning process; however, visualizing how it was going to look was difficult for me since I had never seen a home built of logs. It warmed my heart that Aaron wanted to make sure I liked everything about the house we would live in after we married.

Oh, that road was a challenge! You cannot imagine what it was like to build a road in the middle of a thick forest with only axes and a two-man saw to work with. In addition to the trees that needed clearing, there were large rocks everywhere and a stream that crossed back and forth over the chosen route. After cutting down the trees, the oxen pulled the stumps out one by one, then moved the larger rocks out of the way.

The men cut smaller logs into ten-foot lengths and

laid them down across the road where it was muddiest. The men built culverts from large granite slabs so that the brook ran under the road instead of across it. They dug many cartloads of gravel from a large pit alongside one section of the road and dumped them where needed to make a relatively smooth surface. In the end, the road twisted and turned over and around little hills and huge boulders for a distance of almost a mile until it finally reached the main road.

One afternoon in April Aaron took me to visit the sawmill where all the boards would be prepared for the floor, walls, and roof of our new home. Aaron's uncles, Samuel and Allen gave us a tour and warned us to put our hands over our ears when he put a log through the first saw to demonstrate the process.

There were four saws in a long building – the first trimmed off the slabs, squaring up the log and a second pass cut the log into rough boards. The other saws further trimmed each board to specific widths and lengths and cut the slabs into firewood. (Nothing was wasted.) A planer smoothed each board, and they were then stacked to season for a few months. It was fascinating – I had never seen any big machinery like that at work before and this demonstration gave me a greater appreciation of what was involved with building our house.

While Aaron and his father, brothers, and many friends were preparing for and building our new home and road, Aunt Rebecca and the members of our bee were busy with what they called my "trousseau" — a fancy name for all the clothes, tablecloths, napkins, and quilts that I would need in my new home with Aaron. I protested that we did not need such finery, but they ignored me!

Of course, we worked on a wedding quilt, too. I made up a design using the "Evening Star" block alternating with an appliqué block design that reminded me of pine boughs. The colors were of the woods and flowers that would surround my new home: soft browns, deep green, cream, and a lovely dark brown print for the border.

After I spent weeks piecing the top on Aunt Rebecca's treadle sewing machine, our bee friends came to work together on the hand appliqués and later, the quilting, after I had prepared the sashing and completed piecing the top.

Aunt Rebecca also created what I thought was the most beautiful wedding dress I had ever seen. It was made of white silk and yellow tulle, with many flounces accented with bows made from pale yellow satin ribbons around the skirt and over the bustle. White silk-covered buttons adorned the back and there were tiny pearls setting off the high, lace-trimmed neck. Aunt Rebecca also decorated a lovely bonnet with white lace, silk, and the same tiny pearls and yellow ribbons. The dress was her gift to me. I cried when I put it on for my first fitting. It was breathtaking.

Journal Entry, June 1877

Dearest Mama Tomorrow is my wedding day! I feel lightheaded and cannot sit still. I am impatient for tomorrow to arrive! I thank the good Lord for bringing Aaron and me together and for blessing our union. Just think Mama— starting tomorrow my last name will be Benson. I will be a part of the Benson family. All I have ever dreamed of or wished for is coming to fruition. I feel like the luckiest girl in the world! How I wish you could be here with me, dear Mama. I feel sure you will be looking down upon us tomorrow. Please give us your blessing.

Your incredibly happy daughter, Hannah.

Chapter Nineteen

Our wedding day was lovely and magical. I moved through it with a giddy sense of joy and gratitude. Aaron's father walked me tenderly down the aisle since I had no father of my own, and Lydia and Jane stood up for me at the altar. I felt truly beautiful in the dress that my aunt and Lydia had worked on for months.

I carried a sweet-smelling bouquet of yellow jonquils, narcissus, and white hyacinths from my aunt's garden, with a yellow silk ribbon holding them together. Both Lydia and Jane carried smaller bouquets similar to mine. Flowers of every kind and color filled the church, offered by many of the folks in town. The sweet scent of so many flowers filled the air and flowed around us, contributing to the magical quality of the day.

As I approached Aaron at the altar, my hand resting on William Benson's arm, a feeling of love and pride filled my heart, to be marrying such a handsome and wondrous young man. I almost did not recognize him, all bedecked in his dark suit, shiny new shoes, and high-necked cravat. I was so used to seeing him in his farm clothes that this image of him made me feel as if I were living a fairy tale. Oh, what a dazzling smile met me at the altar. It was all I could do not to throw my arms around his neck at once and not wait for the preacher to pronounce us husband and wife.

After the church service, there was a potluck dinner laid out on the village green. Nearly everyone in town was there and they brought blankets and quilts to sit on, and food to share. A large pit had been dug the day before for a pig roast (a gift from the Benson's), and all that day it cooked over the coals while people took turns turning the spit. The air smelled wonderful with all the succulent aromas from the roasting pig and other delicious foods.

Aunt Rebecca, Lydia, and Rose joined Jane and her parents on quilts near Aaron and me and the rest of the Benson clan. Clara came shyly with little Grace, a toddler now and asked to sit with us as well. Amos and John sat nearby with the three older children. Clara handed me a table scarf that she had appliqued with flowers and vines as a wedding gift. It was exquisite. I was touched and thanked her for her thoughtfulness.

The Bensons, of course, brought many gallons of cider, both sweet and hard, and it was not long before a few of the men grew tipsy and loud. One young man standing near Aaron and me lifted his jug in salute and shouted, with an exaggerated wink:

"Aaron is going to be a lucky man tonight!" Jane's mother, who was standing next to me, shouted back,

"Aaron will be a lucky man all the days of his life!"

Much applause followed this exchange and I blushed in embarrassment.

Soon the fiddles appeared, and everyone cleared space for dancing. I mostly danced with Aaron, of course, but his brothers each wanted a turn and some of the other young men, emboldened perhaps by the cider, also asked for a round. Oh, we danced and danced! Even Mr. Benson took a turn with me in a graceful waltz. Before handing me back to Aaron, he whispered in my ear:

"I am so happy Aaron chose you for his bride," he said. "I am a proud father today. Welcome to our family, Hannah. We are blessed to have you." He gave me a bear hug and I almost cried.

What a festive and happy day that was! As a final surprise gift from the women of our sewing bee, a rented buggy, bedecked with yellow and white ribbons, transported Aaron and me to a small but wonderfully comfortable inn located on the main street of Conway. We stayed there for the first two nights of our marriage. What bliss to be alone together at last and to be as one!

We decided to go on a little adventure the second day to celebrate our marriage. We took a stagecoach to the far side of Mt. Washington where the new Cog Railroad goes up the mountain. We bought two round-trip tickets and settled into one of the front cars of the little train.

Oh my, that WAS an adventure! The track was sometimes way up in the air on wooden trestles that did not look sturdy enough to carry it, and sometimes down among piles of broken rocks and boulders. I was shocked, after the heat of the station at the bottom of the mountain, by the howling wind and cold when we reached the summit. It was as if we had moved from late spring right into winter! I had to hold tight to my hat to keep from blowing away. Fortunately, our hotel hosts had warned us, and we took blankets with us to wrap up in at the top.

However, the high winds had also blown away all the clouds and we could see for miles in every direction from the summit. We saw all the way to our own tiny village and Easton Lake to the south, west into Vermont, east into Maine and all the peaks of the Presidential Range. It was breathtaking.

There was a photographer near the summit house offering to take photos of people for a small fee. We posed against the backdrop of the imposing view for our one and only wedding picture, blankets, and all! I will never forget that day When we returned from our wedding trip, Aaron moved in with me at Aunt R.'s house until our own home was ready. We anticipated moving out there in the early fall.

...

Journal Entry, June 1877

Dearest Mama – Did you ever see any of the mountains in the north? They are truly magnificent. Aaron surprised me, on our honeymoon, with a trip up Mount Washington on the new Cog Railway. I wish you could have come with us. I have to say, the enormity of the mountain and the grandeur of the views overwhelmed me. I felt tiny in a way I never felt before. I clearly saw what a tiny part of this great world of ours I really am. It was almost a relief to come back home (not to mention much warmer), where I can be my accustomed size again and feel right with the world.

Aaron and I are sharing your old bedroom until our new house is ready. We had a new and spacious bed moved in so that now we can be comfortable and not have to share my child-sized bed. How strange it seems to have Aaron by my side every night in my childhood home and my childhood bedroom. It feels sinful, somehow, but at the same time, so right. I am grateful beyond words for the ways in which so many wonderful experiences are falling together in my life!

Your deliriously happy daughter, Hannah

Chapter Twenty

One of Aunt Rebecca's wedding gifts was a large collection of fabric pieces (not just scraps this time, she said to me with a smile). I blushed when I saw that much of the fabric she gave me was perfect for buntings, baby clothes, and tiny blankets.

Sure enough, in early September following our wedding, I began to be sick in the mornings and knew I was with child. When I shyly told Aaron my news, he gave a big whoop and whirled me around the parlor.

"What incredible, lovely news," he said, kissing me and holding me tight. "Let's tell everyone right away!" He could hardly contain himself.

He and I agreed to stay with Aunt Rebecca through the winter until after the baby was born. Spring would be a better time to move.

The months seemed to drag by as I waited anxiously for our little one to arrive. I spent my days sewing but tired easily. Aunt Rebecca and Lydia clucked over me, as I grew bigger and more ungainly. Martha

Benson and Lizzy visited often. Not only would this be OUR first child, it would also be the first grandchild in the Benson family. I am afraid Aaron began to feel a bit like a fifth wheel in a household full of women and constant talk of babies.

When late April came, on a day filled with sunshine and promise, I was more than ready to bear this child. I was impatient with sitting around the house. I had heard many stories of long labors with a first child, but when my pains started, I welcomed them. I was fortunate there were no complications. Mrs. Carter, the midwife, attended me while Aunt Rebecca made sure we had plenty of hot water and clean cloths at hand and she boiled the scissors that would cut the umbilical cord.

Lydia and Rose held me on each side and supported my back when I had to bear down and brought wet clothes to wipe my face. I heard Aaron pacing back and forth outside my room. After several hours of hard labor, a baby boy arrived, squalling loudly. Aaron rushed into the room as soon as he heard the baby cry, and he could hardly contain his pride in his first-born son.

"What a beautiful boy" he whispered in my ear, kissing both the infant and me. "Thank you for giving me a son. Let me hold him." The midwife urged him to be patient a while longer so the baby could be cleaned up and swaddled, then she laid him gently on my breast where he settled sweetly. Finally, Aaron held the baby gingerly in his arms, looking as if he thought the infant might be a crystal vase that could shatter at any moment. He looked at me, his eyes brimming with tears. "I love you so much." he said.

We named the baby Jacob after my father and William after Aaron's father. He was a tiny little thing but had a healthy set of lungs. Baby Jacob had his father's dark brown eyes and a big shock of black hair that looked like it might curl when it grew longer. His face was all squashed and red at first, but to me he was perfection! I could not take my eyes off him.

Mr. and Mrs. Benson arrived a few hours after the birth along with Will, Jesse, Daniel, and Lizzy. They pronounced their first grandson and nephew to be the handsomest baby they had ever seen, and each wanted a turn at holding him. Aaron beamed as family and friends slapped him on the back and congratulated him.

That summer, when Jacob was a few months old, we prepared for our move to our new home. Aaron and his brothers had already taken some of our furniture out to the cabin when the road was dry enough to travel. None-the-less, it was quite an event. Will drove one of the wagons with horses from the Benson farm. Our remaining furniture and personal belongings threatened to overflow the sides of the wagon. Aaron drove the other wagon, drawn by Molly, with me and baby Jacob sitting proudly next to him. Behind us were sacks of potatoes, flour, and other foodstuffs. I had tucked my wedding quilt, carefully wrapped in a blanket for protection, just behind the wagon seat. We decided not to bring out any livestock or chickens to the farm until we built the barn and chicken coop.

The road in was still rough and both wagons

swayed and rattled as the wheels went over rocks and the "corduroy" logs that were laid down where the ground was marshy.

When we finally reached the clearing, I remember being surprised when I saw the roughness of the finished cabin. After living with all the comforts of Aunt Rebecca's house, it was quite an adjustment. However, the cabin was large and full of light and seemed to glow in the sunshine.

We entered by a sturdy front door off a covered porch, which was stacked high with firewood, into a large central room. An enormous fireplace dominated the center of the main room. A pair of graceful hand-forged andirons stood ready, and we soon had a roaring fire going to make us feel welcome. Aaron said he had commissioned Amos to make the andirons, which greatly pleased me.

A brick hearth was laid out in a quarter circle in front of the fireplace, framed in front by a comfortable seating area. Another smaller chimney and hearth stood against the east wall (near the front porch) where a handsome cast iron wood stove awaited winter. A floor to ceiling brick wall flanked the right side of the fireplace with a half wall topped with a built-in bookcase flanking the left side. I saw that Aaron had brought many of my favorite books to the new house, along with others that I did not recognize. My heart was full as I took in his thoughtfulness.

Large windows allowed an expansive view of the lake in front of the cabin, and others the woods on either side. Smaller windows on the back of the cabin looked into the clearing behind. Built-in storage benches surrounded a new pinewood dining table at the far end of the room and a zinc-lined wooden ice chest stood against the outside wall facing the lake. Ice filled the chest, already, and a tube underneath disappeared through a small drain hole in the floor.

"Aaron, this is wonderful." I said and fairly danced around the inviting room.

"Just wait until you see the rest," he said, grinning.

The second room was the kitchen with a large cast iron cook stove and ovens set against the back of the brick wall that flanked the fireplace. Pinewood cupboards hung above a hardwood counter with more cupboards below. A large soapstone sink sat on a very sturdy base on the outside wall under a bank of windows, through which bright sunshine was pouring in. Brand new pots and pans hung from hooks over the stove.

Aaron told me how he and his brothers dug a deep well under the kitchen floor before the flooring went in. A pipe ran from the well through one of the cabinets to a hand pump, which brought fresh cold water directly into the new sink. A long tube ran from the sink drain so that the water could run through the floor, and down the embankment and into a hole filled with sand.

Next to the well and covered with a trap door, there was a wide rectangular space dug out and lined with stones. Aaron had designed it to store apples, winter squash, and root vegetables for the winter, and it was easily accessible from the kitchen.

A third room at the other end of the house held our beautiful new double bed, made by Aaron himself. Lydia had kindly made it up for us in preparation for our arrival. There was just space for a chest of drawers against the wall opposite the foot of the bed and a small, hooked rug and the baby's cradle next to it. My aunt told me that this cradle had rocked her, her brothers, and my mother when they were babies and perhaps generations before that. I loved its rich dark wood and marveled at my own tiny son sleeping in it.

There was a loft above the downstairs rooms with a steep stairway leading up to it ("for the children," Aaron said with a wink). There were wide windows on either end of the loft that gave good light and air circulation. I was almost speechless as Aaron showed me each new room, his face shining, and his voice filled with pride.

I took our wedding quilt out of its protective wrappings and carefully laid it out on our new bed. Then I placed our wedding photo in its frame on one side of the chest and my parents' wedding portrait on the other side. My eyes filled at the sight.

Aaron came up close behind me and, putting his arms around my waist, he kissed the back of my neck.

"We are finally home," he whispered. I turned in his arms.

"Yes, my love, we are finally home!"

When all our helpers were gone, we had a private celebration of new beginnings in a place we could finally call our own.

I soon came to love the honey-colored wood of the beams, walls, and floors, the warmth of the roaring fire on a cold damp night, the way the lake changed colors and texture as the winds and light changed, and the haunting calls of the loons. I especially loved the quiet of the woods that surrounded us.

Although I missed living with Aunt Rebecca, I loved being with Aaron and our infant son without having other people constantly around us. The silence and calm of the woods suited me well. Our life together, in this happy place, was all I ever wanted or had thought of in my dreams.

Chapter Twenty-One

1879

For our second Christmas in our log home, Aaron surprised me with an extravagant gift—a brand new treadle sewing machine made by Mr. Singer's Manufacturing Company! How I had longed for one like my aunt's and suddenly, here it was! I burst into tears at the sight.

Aaron had a mischievous look in his eyes when he left to go into town a few days before Christmas. On Christmas Eve, he told me he had to get something from outside and asked me to close my eyes when he returned, grunting under the heavy load. I remember how he laughed with pleasure at the look on my face when he took the blanket off the sewing machine.

"Oh Aaron," I cried with glee. "Where … How …?" I hardly dared ask.

"Oh, I have my ways" was all he would say on the subject. Suddenly, he scooped me up in his arms and began to dance me around the room. Then I lifted little Jacob from his cradle and the three of us danced around the room until we finally collapsed on the sofa in front of the fire, tears of laughter streaming from our eyes. I could not think, then, of how I could ever be happier than I was at that moment!

The next day I teased and teased Aaron to tell me how he had been able to acquire such a treasure. He finally told me he had saved for many months. Mr. Singer had recently offered a new way to purchase his machines: You could put down whatever you could afford at the time and then pay $.50 a week until it was fully paid. That made it possible for someone like us to purchase such an expensive machine, almost $75.00!

I set the treadle machine in the corner of the large living room with windows to my right and in front of me facing the lake. The view was breathtaking! The bare trees framed the white, snow-covered lake and the mountains beyond looked gray and white under the blue sky. Here and there, a large pine or hemlock tree poked green branches into the white landscape. How quiet and beautiful it was.

In the days that followed, in between my chores, tending the baby, and cooking our meals, I joyfully cut fabric and pieced tiny outfits: little shirts, nightclothes, infant britches. I made diapers and blankets for the crib and finally a quilt from the many colors that remained from all my sewing. The rhythm of the treadle was soothing, and I loved the sound and feel of it. It seemed that in no time I was finished making all those sweet little things for Baby Jacob.

When spring came in 1880, Aaron helped me plant a generous garden a short distance west of the cabin. The previous fall he had cleared the trees and brush from the area followed by a bonfire in the center of the space to get rid of the branches and wood scraps left over from building the cabin. He also cut slender young maple trees and stripped them of their leaves and branches to serve as supports for climbing vegetables.

While little Jacob slept nearby under fine netting, I helped Aaron dig the thick layer of ash into the soil, picking out the rocks as we came to them. Before long, we had quite a tower of rocks beside the garden!

Together we planted hills of summer squash and corn, then pole beans, cucumbers, tomatoes, and other vegetables to grow on Aaron's maple tree poles. I also planted a smaller kitchen garden with lettuce, chard, garlic, and a variety of herbs, including dill for pickling, and my favorite, basil. We would get potatoes and onions at the general store in the village, so we did not plant those. Whatever we could not grow ourselves, we traded for with fresh eggs from the chickens we purchased that summer. We also allowed many of the eggs to hatch so that our flock grew. Eventually, we had chickens to eat and barter, as well as eggs.

Aaron built a small shed and a proper chicken coop and purchased two goats for milk. We named one goat Velvet because her long ears were so soft and silky smooth. The other we named Flopsy because her ears looked so funny, the way they flopped from side to side as she grazed. We also had my horse, Molly, to pull our wagon, and sometimes Aaron rode her into town when he needed something that did not require a wagon.

Aaron had grand plans for our little homestead! First, he would build a barn where he could house more animals and store hay. He wanted to clear pastures, build fences. He dreamed of an addition to our cabin and perhaps a wide veranda on the front facing the lake. There seemed no end to his plans! However, he was patient.

"All in good time, my sweet," he would say.

After he took care of the necessities, Aaron built a wooden bench on a small rise near the cabin. It had a clear view of the lake and the surrounding mountains and was a lovely spot to sit and take in the beauty of our little world. Sometimes, of an evening, after Jacob was in bed, Aaron and I would sit on the bench together and watch the sky turn from dusky blue to pink and peach, to purple and finally to gray as the sun set behind the western peaks. Sometimes we sat quietly, holding hands, no need to speak. At other times, we spoke softly about our dreams and plans for the future.

One evening Aaron held me close as we sat, watching the night creep over us. He said,

"If ever there comes a time, Hannah, when I cannot be with you, come, and sit on this bench and I will be here beside you. I will hear your voice when you call my name, and I will see your dear face. You will always be in my heart."

"And you in mine, my Love," I whispered. "We are one. We will never part."

Journal Entry, June 1880

Dearest Mama — We ad quite a scare last night! We woke up to a great ruckus coming from the chickens. Aaron grabbed his rifle and we rushed out in our nightclothes to see what had caused such a fuss. There was a hole in the side of the chicken coop and in the dim light, we could just see the bushy tail of a large fox disappearing into the woods. One of our chickens was missing and there were feathers everywhere. Thank goodness, none of the others seemed to be injured.

I never really thought about the animals in our woods who could do us or our livestock harm. We frequently see deer, rabbits, and wild turkeys but never anything dangerous. I guess we will have to build a stronger pen and be more alert. Little Jacob thought the whole episode was a great adventure. We will have to teach him how to stay safe as well.

You should see him, Mama—he is growing up straight and tall. I almost wish he would not grow up quite so fast.

Your loving but nervous daughter, Hannah

Chapter Twenty-Two

1880

One afternoon in August, when it was too hot to work in the garden, Aaron announced it was time for me to learn to swim. Jacob, now an adventurous toddler, was off visiting his Grandma Benson so we had some precious time to ourselves. Looking after an active two-year-old is exhausting.

"My Pa taught me and each of my brothers how to swim when we were young so we would be safe to go out in the canoe with him fishing," Aaron said. "I think it's high time you learned to swim."

"Swim!" I exclaimed. "How are we going to accomplish that?" I felt scared but also excited by the idea.

"You'll see," he said, winking at me. Then we walked down the short path to the lakeshore where Aaron kept our canoe tied up.

"The water is quite shallow here, Hannah, so don't be nervous. Of course, you will need to take off your dress." He laughed when he saw the look on my face. "No one will see you but me!" he said in a teasing voice.

I took off everything except my shift and he peeled down to his undergarments. Then I stepped gingerly into the water with Aaron holding my hand. The rocks on the bottom were slippery with moss but Aaron held me steady. The water was unexpectedly chilly at first but with the intense heat, it was a welcome relief.

Aaron led me deeper and deeper into the water while I squealed with laughter and pretended fright, and soon I was "swimming", as Aaron held his arms under me. Oh, what fun we had that afternoon!

It was not long before we were practicing swimming as often as Granny Benson or Lizzy could watch Jacob. Jacob loved his visits to the Benson farm as much as they enjoyed having him. When Aaron and I returned to fetch him at the end of the day and visit for a while, he would regale us (as only a toddler can) with "stories" of his fun playing with his uncles and with Lizzy and the sweets his Granny gave him. Even his Grandpa got into it, riding little Jacob around on his shoulders. How lucky I was to have such loving in-laws.

Aaron also took me out in the canoe to explore the lake and I remembered the very first time I came to this beautiful place with him. Such a sweet memory.

We soon discovered masses of high bush blueberries all around the lakeshore. By the third week in August, they were full ripe and the two of us, with Jacob strapped carefully in the canoe, took buckets, and jars out on the water and filled them all with this rich bounty. There were so many blueberries we could have filled the entire canoe with them if we wanted to. We gave some of them to little Jacob and he laughed happily at the sweet taste.

"More, Mama, more!" he begged, and of course, I could not refuse him.

On one of our excursions on the lake, we saw a pair of loons with a baby chick swimming nearby. It was just outside the cove where the path from the Benson farm met the lake. Usually, we only saw the loons at a distance. These were not more than twenty feet from our canoe. One of them dove and suddenly popped up right next to me. I was so startled I almost tipped us into the water! It is surprising how big the Loons are when you can see them up close, but they quickly dive out of sight if they get nervous and pop up again far away.

"How can they stay underwater for so long?" I asked Aaron.

"The loons can stick the tip of their beaks just out of the water to draw breath. That way they can travel long distances without being seen," he said.

We often heard them calling to each other, both day and night. They have a soft, laughing call when all is well and a quick hoot to locate each other at a distance. Sometimes, when they feel threatened or are in distress, they have an almost diabolical high-pitched shrieking call that sends shivers up my spine. The sounds they make are eerie yet mesmerizing at the same time.

With all the blueberries we gathered, I baked

blueberry pies, muffins, and pancakes as well as making jam. When I finished, Aaron and I decided to take Jacob and as many vegetables and baked goods as we could into the village to barter and for a visit. Once again, the wagon bumped and rattled along our road and I wished for the thousandth time that we could make it smoother.

We traded at the general store for much-needed staples and had a nice long visit with Jane and her mother and later with Aunt Rebecca, Lydia, and Rose at their house. Everyone exclaimed over little Jacob, how fast he was growing, how long his curly black hair was getting, and his big dimples when he smiled, and so on. Jacob was starting to walk and amused all of us as he toddled bravely first toward one then another, and then suddenly plopped down on his bottom. He would look surprised and then giggle, which of course got the rest of us laughing. My fearless and adorable boy.

Our friends urged us to visit more often than just on Sundays and market days and we promised we would, but sometimes that was difficult with all we had to do on our small farm.

Journal Entry August 1880

Dearest Mama— Can you believe it? I can swim! Aaron taught me how. He has the patience of a saint, that man. He held me up while I floundered around in the water before I finally got the knack of it. I think I can finally swim on my own, but it is more fun with Aaron holding me, so I pretend I still need his support. I blush to tell you what I wear when we swim—just my shift! It would be nice if we could swim without any clothes at all, but I am too embarrassed to do that. Aaron tells me I am silly to feel that way since no one else is on the lake to see us. Maybe I will get brave next summer. Do you think that would be wicked?

The lake is so beautiful with all the trees on the shore and the hills and mountains beyond. When we are out on the water, it feels as if we are the only people in the whole world. I do wish so that you could see how happy Aaron and I our beautiful baby boy are together, and how fast is growing. I feel so blessed.

Your loving daughter, Hannah

Chapter Twenty-Three

1880-1881

That fall, when we had been in the cabin for just over two years, Aaron's brothers, Jesse, Daniel, and Will, came once again to help cut trees and fashion the large beams that would be the sills and huge square posts for our barn. Samuel and Allen Benson made all the flooring and siding for the barn at their sawmill, just as they had for our cabin. I enjoyed watching the men work together as a team— they worked almost in unison for hours at a time and made great progress. It was quite a sight.

When spring 1881 came and Jacob was three years old, the barn was ready to raise. I remember how all the able-bodied men in the village and surrounding area came to help, bringing their wives and children. The women prepared food and drink for the workers.

All day, the men heaved, pushed, and pounded until finally, at dusk, a cheer went up as the men pounded the last peg into the last beam and the frame of the barn stood tall and strong. They laid the floor, as well, leaving only the outside walls, the hayloft and roof to complete.

The women spread platters of roasted meat on long plank tables, along with fresh-made bread, cheese, and jugs of cider for the hungry crew. I spread one of my pieced coverlets on a table and several of the women admired it: the beautiful colors, the pretty block designs, the fine stitching. I felt quite embarrassed by their admiration. After that, of course, they wanted to know how I pieced the top with such tiny stitches.

When I told them about my treadle machine, they all wanted to crowd into our living room to see it. They oohed and ahhed over it, having never seen one before and were fascinated by how the machine worked to make such tiny, even stitches They also remarked about the ingenuity of the foot pedal and flywheel. In those days, sewing machines were still quite rare and my machine and my Aunt Rebecca's two were still the only treadle sewing machines in the village.

The women also exclaimed over Jacob, who was obviously enjoying all the attention. He was not at all shy and ran around from person to person to say hello. He was quite the little flirt! Everyone thought he was adorable.

"Look at how sturdy he is," one would say or "How much like your Aaron he looks!" "He is quite the talker, isn't he," another said.

The men teased Aaron about what a fine strapping young son he had sired. "Next time a beautiful baby girl to rival your beautiful bride!" someone called. I blushed with pleasure.

The men drank hard cider and Joe Skinner brought out his fiddle while another musician tuned his mandolin and the young folk jumped up for the first dance. They quickly formed two lines, the women facing the men for a reel. Aaron grabbed my hand and pulled me, protesting, into the dance. He grinned at me across the line as we moved forward and back in time to the lively music.

I remember thinking, "I must be the luckiest woman in the world!"

By early September, after several weeks of working alongside his brothers once again, the siding and roof of the barn were finished. Aaron brought a load of hay from his father's farm and stored it in the loft and Molly and the goats moved into their spacious new home. When we were finally alone and Jacob was fast asleep, Aaron and I had our own private celebration of all we had accomplished.

Journal Entry, September 1881

Dearest Mama— I am up to my elbows canning tomatoes and pickling cucumbers. Sometimes I wonder if the work will ever end. It's funny, though—even when I am exhausted after a day of working in the garden and then in the kitchen preparing food for the winter months, all the while trying to keep up with Jacob, I would not trade places with anyone! This is right where I belong. Jacob is running all around now and talking a blue streak. I wish I could borrow some of his energy. He is a joy and keeps me laughing. He comes up with the funniest words and phrases when he gets excited and tries to tell me something and does not get the words quite right. His questions are endless – he wants to know everything! When I mentioned this to Aunt Rebecca a few days ago, she said this is just the way I was as a child. I hope I did not wear her out the way Jacob does me sometimes. I am so proud of Aaron and so grateful for the many folks who came to help us with the barn raising. There were more than fifty people here and we had a grand celebration after the frame was up.

Your loving but exhausted daughter, Hannah

Chapter Twenty-Four

1881-1882

In late October, I again experienced the morning nausea and the swelling tenderness of my breasts. I had missed two of my "monthlies" but waited a few more days to be sure before I whispered into Aaron's ear,

"By late winter there will be another babe, a girl, this time, I think."

Aaron threw his arms around me in a bear hug. Then he chuckled and teased

"What makes you so sure it will be a girl?"

"I just know," I replied, with a grin.

Sure enough, I was right! The following June, when my time was near, I sent Aaron into town to fetch the midwife, Aunt Rebecca, Lydia, and Rose.

This time, my labor was more difficult, and I was grateful for their support. Near supper time of the second day, I delivered a beautiful little girl. She had white-blond fuzz on the top of her head and the bluest eyes! We decided to name her Sarah Rachel.

When Aunt Rebecca saw her, she exclaimed that the baby was the very image of my own mother when she was born. She could not get over the likeness. I thought in my heart "I hope she will be luckier in her life than my mother was!" However, the thought was fleeting; it was borne away by the joy I felt when I held my perfect baby girl.

Aaron could not get enough of baby Sarah and sat rocking her in his arms while I rested. Later, Lydia brought Jacob, not quite four then, in to meet his new little sister. He was intrigued and wanted to hold her but had to content himself with patting her gently while she slept.

We were so happy then, Aaron and me and our growing family! Many times, in the days that followed Sarah's birth, I had to suddenly stop whatever I was doing and say "Thank you, Lord, for your many blessings." I did not know what was yet to come.

Soon after baby Sarah's birth, Aaron presented me with an eight-week-old puppy, a small ball of black and white fluff. He was funny and endearing and won my heart immediately. We decided to call him "Sunny" because he seemed so full of joy just to be alive. He was the offspring of two of the sheepherding dogs that Aaron's parents raised to keep track of their sheep and cows.

These dogs had fascinated me from the first time I saw them working. Their speed, agility, and ability to keep the sheep where they were supposed to be with just a whistle or a hand sign from Will or Jesse astonished me and I marveled at how, every evening, they brought in the cows in for milking without being "told." They even kept track of the chickens! Aaron joked that with the increase in the number of people and animals on our little farm, we clearly needed a smart dog to keep us all organized and in line!

Aaron began training Sunny right away and he was a fast learner. I was amazed at how quickly he learned to do his business outside the cabin, to sit and stay when commanded, to come when called and all the other important things a dog must know, especially deep in the woods the way we were. The woods around us were full of deer, and we did not want Sunny chasing them. However, there were also bears, foxes, wolverines, and fishers nearby who could easily snatch up a puppy and eat him before anyone knew he was missing! Sunny had strict orders never to leave the area around the house and barn unless he was with Aaron.

Sunny bonded quickly with both of us but Aaron was his favorite. He became Aaron's shadow and followed him everywhere. It was not long before he was well acquainted with the goats and chickens and was teaching THEM a thing or two!

Journal Entry, July 1882

Dearest Mama—We have another sweet addition to our family. Her name is Sarah Rachel. I wish you could see her. She is not fussy at all and sleeps a good part of the time so I can get some rest. I hope she will grow up to be as beautiful as you were.

Jacob is funny—he is not quite sure yet what to make of the tiny creature who is taking up most of his Mama's attention right now. I am sure he will grow to love her as much as we do. Sunny is three months old now and a great addition to the family. He has been eager to meet Sarah also, and today we let him sniff her to get used to her scent. Before we knew it, he gave her a big wet kiss right across her face and she opened her eyes in surprise and smiled! A new baby is such a wondrous thing. Our family is truly blessed.

Your loving and contented daughter, Hannah

One afternoon, a few weeks after Sarah was born, I went into town with the baby to get some much-needed supplies at the general store and, of course, to visit and to show off the beautiful new member of our family.

"How wonderful to see you up and about so soon after your confinement," Mrs. McNally said. "And what a sweet little babe you have here!"

Jane, too, was pleased to see us. "I missed you these past weeks," she confided as she admired little Sarah. "I have something to tell you." Her face flushed. "Oh Hannah, look at this" she said holding out her left hand. On her fourth left finger, there was a lovely ring set with a ruby in the center and two small diamonds on either side.

"I have a suitor!" she said. "He has asked me to marry him, and I said yes!"

"When did this happen," I asked surprised. "Why didn't you tell me you were being courted?"

"It happened quite suddenly," Jane said, "and you haven't come into town since before the baby was born. Never mind. His name is Samuel. His father owns a large supply store in Conway with whom we do business. He has been coming here every couple of weeks to deliver goods to our store and we talk a little before he has to leave. This last time, he got up his nerve to ask me if I wanted to go walking with him. I did. And he asked me!"

"That is wonderful!" I said, giving her a big hug. "How do your parents feel about him?"

"They are thrilled," she said. "I think they have been worried I might meet someone and move away. Samuel is already in almost the same business and we will be able to continue running the store together when my parents are no longer able to. His older brother will inherit his father's store. This is a perfect solution."

"Such wonderful news," I exclaimed. "I am so happy for you." When she asked me to be her matron of honor at their wedding, of course I said yes!

They were married the following spring and my heart rejoiced for the happiness of my best friend.

...

Journal Entry, June 1882

Dearest Mama - My heart is full. Jane has married a wonderful young man named Samuel Morrison. I stood up with them at the wedding and I could not be more proud. Sam is a genuinely nice young man. He is tall and very thin — to look at them side by side is quite amusing for Jane is quite plump. Of course, no one would dare say so. Sam is much quieter than Jane is, but they seem to suit each other perfectly in much the same way Jane's parents do. The two of them are renting a small house near the general store until they can afford to buy or build a house of their own.

Sam has all kinds of ideas for how to expand and improve the store, but he is being careful not to overstep his position as long as Jane's parents still run it. I know we will all be good friends through the years.

Do you remember my friend Clara? I have not written of her for a while. Her oldest son, George, is seventeen now — seems hardly possible he is almost grown. He has been learning the blacksmith trade from his Papa. Amos has been poorly lately and cannot work as hard as he used to. Billy and Sallie Mae are doing well in school, and Grace, also, she just started last fall. Clara has slow but steady work from some of the women in the village, but in summer, when the rich visitors arrive, she is remarkably busy. I am happy for her. I wish I could see her more often but, at least I still see her every month at our bee meetings.

Your loving daughter Hannah

Apparently, love and marriage were in the air. Rose confided to me not long after Jane and Samuel were married, that she, too, was in love. To my great astonishment and pleasure, she told me that Daniel Benson had been courting her for some time. They had known each other since early childhood and had gone to school together but with a seven-year difference in their ages, it was not until recently that they realized the strength of their feelings for each other.

Rose's dream was to one day own a small inn near the lake where she could spend her days cooking and taking care of guests. This idea suited Daniel fine. He was tired of helping on his parent's farm with no prospects of inheriting one of his own. He and Rose could raise enough fresh produce and keep a few chickens to feed their guests.

Rose asked Lydia and me to stand with her at their wedding. I felt honored to do so when they wed in September of 1882.

My Aunt Rebecca joined with Daniel's parents in a wedding gift of a down payment on a large farmhouse with several acres of land on a hill overlooking the lake. It was just a short distance from the center of the village and the railroad station. After a brief wedding trip, Rose and Daniel began working on transforming the house into an inn. I was thrilled to see their dreams coming true!

Chapter Twenty-Five

1883

As I said before, life can be cruel. One year later, in June, when Jacob was almost five and baby Sarah already one, I once again felt the morning sickness and my breasts began to swell. I was elated! However, it was too soon to be sure, so I said nothing to Aaron. He had been off all day with his brothers working in the woods. I remember the black flies were fierce that spring and I could not understand how the men could stand logging in the forest in the heat with all those vicious little flies!

I had been planting the garden most of the morning, with Jacob's help, and again that afternoon until my back was so sore, I had to stop. I was almost three months along and felt overcome with the heat and the black flies. (It seems strange how you can sometimes remember minute details just before something terrible happens.)

In late afternoon, Aaron's brothers appeared with Molly and the wagon. Behind them, on horseback, were Rose and Lizzy Benson, their faces stricken. I knew immediately that something was very wrong. The looks on the men's faces told me everything.

I stood tall and calm. "Where is Aaron?" I asked. "Tell me what has happened." Rose and Lizzy ran over to me and Aaron's brothers stood with their hats in their hands, not knowing how to say the words. Lizzy was crying. Rose was holding my hand. Daniel finally stammered,

"I am so sorry, Hannah! We all are. There has been a terrible accident in the woods."

I asked again, raising my voice. "What happened? I want to know everything! And where is Aaron?" Will turned his head toward Molly and the wagon.

"He's in there, Hannah." He choked. "We thought he was clear. We were bringing down a big tree hung up in another one. We had it tied up with chains and everything, but suddenly it snapped at the base and kicked off in the wrong direction. We yelled at Aaron, but it was too late. He was pinned by one of the branches. Oh Jesus, Hannah, we wish this had never happened!" He began to sob.

I walked toward the wagon, feeling numb. Aaron lay on the floorboards under an old blanket. He looked gray and a deep hollow sunk downwards where his chest should have been. Blood soaked the blanket. I touched his face. It was cold. My Aaron, my beloved husband, had already flown. He was not here. From a great distance, somewhere inside my head, I heard the words, "It is God's will." I did not weep.

"Godspeed, my love," I whispered, and turned

away.

Journal Entry, June 1883

Oh, Mama—my heart is shattered into a million pieces!
I cannot think, feel, or even write except to say God has taken
my beloved from me. It may be God's will, but it is too cruel!
I do not know how I can live.

Hannah

I was in a dream from which I could not wake. I vaguely remember a funeral at the Benson Farm. What had been my Aaron now lay in the ground in the family plot. Many people came from the village to pay their respects and to offer words of sympathy and encouragement to me and to his parents and siblings.

I also vaguely remember refusing to leave our little farm. Lydia stayed with me to help care for Jacob and Sarah, do the gardening, and prepare the meals. Will and Jesse came to help cut and split firewood for the winter, care for the animals and do some of the other heavy chores. I felt suspended between heaven and earth, unable to function rationally. Still, I had not wept.

In November, when I was five months along, my aunt and other friends and family insisted I move back into town. Reluctantly I went to live with my aunt again. All our animals, even Sunny, went to the

Benson's farm where they could be cared for. Others arranged everything for me. I was sleepwalking.

Aunt Rebecca, Rose, and Lydia took great care of my little ones and me. I was told later that I gave up eating and became severely withdrawn, staring off into a place where no one could reach me. I would not touch my sewing machine. Even Jacob and baby Sarah could not penetrate the walls that surrounded me although I learned later that I did hold them and rock them sometimes. I remember nothing about that and feel guilty that I was unable to love them during that time.

My aunt told me months later that I would sit for hours during the day staring blankly out the window. She tried to entice me with tasty morsels of food or with swatches of soft velvet and rich satin. I would take them in my hands and let them drop on the floor. The doctor came and gave me teas and potions. Nothing touched me. At night, when I could sleep, the terrible nightmares of my childhood returned full force. I fell endlessly through the darkness or crawled in panic through a narrow tunnel that had no way out. Sometimes I was in a large empty house, going from room to room and up many flights of stairs, searching and searching but finding no one. All the doors and windows locked from the outside and I could not escape. Aunt Rebecca or Lydia came to me when they heard me cry out.

One night in early December, I awakened from my fitful sleep with tearing pains in my belly. My sheets and bedclothes were soaked. I vaguely understood that I was in labor and that it was much too soon, and I screamed for help. I learned later that Aunt Rebecca had summoned the doctor as well as a midwife to attend me, but I remember nothing of what happened during that sad night. I did not learn until the next day that my baby was born dead. I did not look at him. I was too numb to cry. Soon after that, Mr. and Mrs. Benson came to see me. They took the baby, still unnamed, to lie beside his father. Other friends and neighbors came to offer their condolences and to wish me well, but I was hardly aware of them.

During the long dark months that followed, I eventually began to stir and grow restless. As my physical strength returned, my aunt urged me to go to church with her on Sundays and to the monthly church socials. I usually refused. However, with Lydia at home to tend to the children, I occasionally relented to appease my aunt.

I spoke to no one at church and always went right home after the service. At the socials, I stood quietly against a wall, trying to be as inconspicuous as possible while the music played, and others danced. Occasionally Mr. and Mrs. Benson or one of Aaron's brothers would try to speak to me but I did not want to see them yet. My women friends approached me, but the men knew enough to stay away.

I occasionally agreed to go to the monthly quilting bee meetings. However, I could not bring myself to take up needle and thread to work on someone's quilt. Mrs. Benson came occasionally, and I saw her struggling with her own grief. Sometimes, we just sat together holding hands, not saying a word. I do think being among my quilting friends was a comfort and I began to feel the great gray fog begin to lift off my spirit a little.

By March, I began to take long walks alone along the country roads surrounding our village. I took no notice of where I was going, just walked until I was exhausted. Sometimes my walks took me out the road that led to the Benson's farm. I would suddenly realize where I was going and would impulsively turn back towards town.

As I walked, I gradually became aware of the scents and sounds of early spring—the gurgle of snow-fed brooks coming off the mountains and the rivulets of water trickling from the remaining patches of snow. I saw tiny buds beginning to form on the branches above me, and, for the first time in many months, I heard birds chirping and the little "chip-chipping" of the wood's animals.

It is funny about life—it goes on whether or not you want it to. The world still turns; the sun rises every morning; the seasons change. I began to awaken as if from a long sleep and my little world began to come back into focus, bit by bit.

It was time to return to my real home, the little farm that Aaron and I built together. Aunt Rebecca protested, of course, but I won out. However, I did agree to have Aaron's little sister Lizzy come and stay with me for a while to help with the children and chores. She had grown up into a sweet young woman and was a great help to me. Lydia visited often when she could but kept busy at home making dresses for Aunt Rebecca's customers. Will and Jesse promised to bring the animals out to the farm and to visit often to help with the heavy work.

Jacob had constant questions as I packed our

belongings into our wagon and hitched Molly up to lead us home. Would Sunny be there? Would the goats be there? How about the chickens?

"Maybe Papa will be there waiting for us," Jacob said hopefully.

"No dearest, Papa will not be there," I said, as I stifled the sudden clenching pain I felt in my chest.

Chapter Twenty-Six

1884

There was much to do when we returned. There were repairs to make to the fences and barn and cleaning up the many branches brought down by the heavy snows of winter. There was the garden to prepare and plant. It was wonderful to have Lizzy there and I appreciated Will and Jesse's assistance as well.

I do not remember much from that time but I know that I kept myself busy from morning until nightfall so I would not have to think or feel. It was only in the quiet of the night, after Lizzy and the children were asleep, that I felt the emptiness. I would angrily push it away to fall into a fitful sleep.

In all the months at Aunt Rebecca's house, my sewing machine stood untouched. For our return to the cabin, it was carefully padded and wedged into the wagon and carried into the house. It still sat covered and neglected in the corner of the large living room. I did not have the ambition or energy to think about it.

Sunny was happy to be home again and was his old playful self, most of the time, but I saw him moving from one part of our little farm to another as if he were searching for something. I finally realized he was searching for Aaron! He missed Aaron as much as the children did! He moped for a long time but eventually he seemed to accept Aaron's absence and began to shadow Jacob. (How lucky dogs are, I mused one afternoon, living only in the present moment, no painful memories of the past or fears for the future.)

When we first came home, Little Sarah often asked when she would see her Papa again. Both she and Jacob were too young to grasp fully what had happened and it was too painful for me to try to explain. Sarah became clingy and begged to sit in my lap, or she would wrap her little arms around my legs and whine, begging me to pick her up, but I did not have much time or patience for sitting or holding her.

Sarah and Jacob were both sad for a long time, moving listlessly through each day, doing only what was required of them. I did not have the energy or courage to try to ease their pain or give them the loving attention they so clearly needed. Eventually, they began to play again and to help where they could with some of the chores, but the joy had left them.

Spring and summer passed slowly, it seemed, and fall arrived crisp and cool. Lizzy stayed on until we finished harvesting the garden and putting food up for the winter. Then she returned to her parent's house to help her mother. I missed her sorely but also enjoyed the solitude at night, especially after the children went to bed.

During the fall, Will came often to cut and stack firewood for the months to come and to bring hay from the Benson farm for Molly and the goats. He also brought cider and loaves of fresh bread or an apple pie that his mother baked for the children and me. Sometimes, the children begged him to stay for dinner and visit for a while after he finished his chores, and I could see he wanted to, but I was still not in a visiting mood. I was grateful for his company, but I was also grateful when he went home again each evening.

One afternoon I caught Will staring at me from across the garden. As soon as he saw me meet his stare, he blushed and immediately looked away. I was not sure how to respond to him and was relieved when he went home. Some days later, he lingered after he finished his work, and asked if he could stay awhile.

"I wish to speak to you, to ask…," he said lamely, his voice trailing off. He stood awkwardly, his hat in his hands, unsure what else to say. Will was a man of few words, but I could read the question in his eyes.

"Will, I so appreciate all you are doing for us," I said. "You have been a true friend. However, seeing you every day is also confusing. You remind me too much of Aaron. It is both comforting and painful at the same time. I hope you understand." I could see the hurt and disappointment in his face. "I am sorry, Will," I said softly, putting my hand on his arm. "I am not ready yet."

"I understand," he said softly, turning away, his shoulders slumped.

I moved back into town to live with Aunt Rebecca for the winter and the animals went again to the Benson's farm. I was more aware of my surroundings this time and was able to participate in the running of the household and taking care of my children. Nonetheless, I still felt, some days, as if I were sleepwalking through my life.

Aunt Rebecca insisted I get out to see my friends, to attend bee meetings, if only for the company, and to attend church. I knew it would do me good to go, but I just did not have the energy most of the time. My sewing machine still sat untouched. In all the months since that terrible day, I had yet to shed a single tear.

The following spring (1885), I returned, as before, to our farm on the lake. I mechanically planted the garden, spent hours weeding and cleared areas where ferns had moved into the open field. There was so much to do—I was busy from dawn until dusk and fell exhausted into bed every night. Thankfully, the nightmares of the past came to haunt me less often.

Will continued to come out to help with some of the heavy work. It was awkward, at times, but I was glad to see him. Rose and Lydia both visited as well. I enjoyed their company but was again grateful when they went home.

Late that summer I was standing in my garden, leaning on my hoe, and resting for a moment. I ached with weariness and my back hurt, but it was a good feeling, a feeling of satisfaction and of a job well done.

I listened to the laughter of the children playing among the rows of corn, their high-pitched giggles and shrieks rising above the silken tassels. Sunny ran back and forth along the edge of the garden, barking, wanting to be part of the game. He knew better than to come into the garden!

I watched Jacob and Sarah fondly as I continued my weeding, catching a glimpse of first one, and then the other, as they darted in and out of the cornstalks. I felt peaceful, which was the closest to happy I had been in a long time. It was good to see Jacob playing this way. It had been hard to watch his sorrow and not be able to help. He carried far more weight on his shoulders than a seven-year-old should have to bear. Sarah, at three, seemed oblivious now to all that had happened. She no longer clung to me and was a constant delight. "My sunshine girl," I used to call her.

As I continued weeding. Thoughts of the past came to me, unbidden. Snippets of memories passed through my mind, like soft clouds on a summer day. Aaron and me, growing up together, running through a field after church trying to catch butterflies or Aaron carrying my books home from school. Visiting Jane at her parents' general store and drinking in the delicious smells of fresh baked bread and pipe tobacco. The farm where Aaron's family lived, the smell of apple blossoms, making cider with Aaron's family in the fall, and sliding down the long hill in the fresh snow, shrieking with laughter.

Suddenly I shivered as a whisper of wind and a small chill brought me back to the present. I began to gather up my gardening tools and brushed the dust off my long dress. The heavy braid that hung down my back had begun to unravel, and I brushed a loose strand of hair out of my eyes. The sky was darkening early.

"Looks like rain's coming," I thought absently. "The garden needs a good soaking." No rain had fallen in almost two weeks and the ripening vegetables looked parched.

I moved toward the small barn where Molly and the two goats waited patiently near the fence for their nightly feeding. Molly whickered softly and nuzzled my hand when I approached, looking for a carrot, or a piece of apple. "Not right now, girl," I said gently to my old friend as I led the animals into the barn. While I was pulling down a fresh supply of hay, I mused about what my life was like without Aaron. How long ago was it? It was more than two years now. Black fly season. A tree falling wrong ... I was surprised to realize I had to think to remember how long it had been.

I brought myself back with a start. It was mid-August now. The corn would be full ripe in another week or so. The tomatoes were starting to turn crimson. I had been canning beans for several weeks already and was running out of ways to use the explosion of summer squash.

It was hard work keeping up with the garden and the animals as well as tending to the children and keeping house, but I enjoyed being busy. On my rare trips into town, Aunt Rebecca hinted that I should stop being so stubborn and remarry.

"There are lots of fine young men available, strong ones, hard workers," she would say. "I have seen the way some of them look at you, especially Will. It is not fitting for you to be living all alone with the children so far from town."

"Nonsense," I would reply, emphatically, feeling a little annoyed. "We are doing just fine on our own!" I knew my Aunt Rebecca meant well, but I did not like her meddling.

Sometimes, though, when I paused in my work, I felt a deep ache of loneliness. It would be nice, I occasionally allowed myself to admit, to have someone to talk to and to help with the chores and the children. Maybe a man … But that was too painful to think about and I would shut out the thought as soon as it arrived.

As I left the barn, I felt the wind strengthen and the first drops of rain began to fall. I called to Sunny and told the children to wash up while I returned to the cabin to prepare dinner.

By the time I tucked Sarah and Jacob into bed, the storm had struck full force. The wind and rain hurtled down the lake, churning the water into white froth. When it reached our cove at the south end, it slammed into the woods, whipping trees around in a frenzied dance. Flashes of jagged lightening cut the night sky and thunder crashed so close to the house that the log walls shuddered. Sunny retreated under my bed, whimpering, and the children did not want to be alone.

The storm raged around us for three days and three nights with hardly a respite. Inside our little fortress, I kept a fire blazing in the large fireplace, and two kerosene lamps shone brightly to ward off the darkness and fury of the storm. The windows rattled ominously, and the walls vibrated while all around the cabin I heard trees snapping like matchsticks and the wind moaned and howled.

Sarah and Jacob were frightened and huddled under one of my patchwork quilts near the fire. I comforted them as best I could, reading them stories, giving them hot soup, holding them when the sound of falling trees set them crying again. I was frightened, too. I had never experienced a storm this fierce. At every moment, I expected a tree to come down through the roof onto the three of us.

I tried to get out to the barn several times to tend to the animals, but each time, the wind beat me back. Rain soaked my long and wrinkled dress and soot from the fireplace and bits of bark covered it from the logs I carried in from the woodpile on the porch. My hair, uncombed for three days, hung in damp strands down my back. I did not notice. I had hardly slept or eaten since the first night of the storm. I was beyond exhaustion. Finally, unable to do any more, I fell into a fitful doze, my sleep haunted by nightmares of monsters and flying trees.

I woke near dawn of the fourth day to an eerie silence. The rain had stopped, and the air was still. A heavy mist enveloped everything in a shroud. No birds sang. I stepped cautiously outside to survey the damage. Sarah and Jacob, energized by their long confinement, came bursting past me, their fear forgotten. Sunny danced and barked his excitement.

Look, Ma," Sarah cried gleefully, picking up an armload of sodden pinecones. They were strewn everywhere among the branches and shingles that littered the ground. Bricks from the two chimneys lay in piles, haphazardly near the house, and the remains of the porch roof were wedged incongruously between two miraculously intact trees.

"Oh, Ma! Come quick!" Jacob shouted from the clearing out back. A giant hemlock tree had narrowly missed crushing the cabin and now lay across my beautifully cultivated vegetable garden. Cornstalks, beanpoles, and the elephant ears of summer squash lay twisted and flattened in the mud. The ground was red with the blood of mangled tomatoes.

The roots of the huge tree lifted jagged fingers towards the sky. The upper branches disappeared through the roof of the small barn.

"Oh, dear God" I cried, running to the barn with Jacob and Sarah close behind me. I could hear the bleating of one of the goats and followed the sound. Velvet stood cowering in the corner of one of the stalls, frightened but unhurt. Flopsy lay nearby, crushed under the tip of the fallen hemlock. The bedraggled chickens ran everywhere, pecking amongst the debris.

"Lord be merciful," I whispered. Molly was nowhere in sight. "Molly! Where are you, girl? Molly, come here!" Frantic, I ran out of the barn and around to the back. There was Molly, standing in the middle of what had been the fenced-in paddock, munching on sodden grass through branches of a fallen maple tree.

"Oh, Molly, thank God you are all right!" I leaned against the warm, strong body of my old friend, and buried my face in her course hair. Tears of exhaustion, relief, and rage began to prick behind my eyes.

"No," I thought impatiently, "I will not give in to this! I can't!" But, in spite of myself, tears, held in for so many months, came unbidden, rolling over me in great waves. I cried in long tearing sobs, digging my fingers into Molly's mane. I cried for Aaron, I cried for my fatherless children, my stillborn son, for the dead goat, for my beautiful garden, for all the trees I had loved which now lay uprooted and broken in a tangled mess. I cried, finally, for myself until there were no more tears. Sarah and Jacob, frightened, stood nearby with their arms around Velvet, not knowing what to do. Sunny poked me with his soft nose, nuzzling against me. I put my hand down to stroke his head absently.

After what seemed like an eternity, I became aware of the sound of the children sniffling nearby. I called to them softly and scooped them into my arms when they came running.

"Mama's all right now," I said, kissing their soft hair. "Everything will be all right!" I walked slowly, wearily, toward the lake, and sank down on the bench Aaron had made for us so long ago, seeking solace in the quiet. The water was utterly still, the color of slate. The heavy mist was lifting here and there in wisps, slowly revealing the trees and rocks that lined the far shore. The hills beyond were still swallowed up in darkness.

"Oh Aaron," I whispered. "Where are you?"

Suddenly something in the far distance caught my eye. I came instantly alert. A canoe, barely visible, moved out of the mist. It was too far to make out any detail, but it appeared to be heading our way.

"Come, children. Let's go into the house," I said firmly. Sarah and Jacob, with Sunny close behind, instantly obeyed, knowing that tone in my voice. I lifted the old rifle down from its perch above the fireplace and checked to be sure that it was loaded.

"Stay inside, now, hear? And don't open the door until I say you can."

"Yes, Ma," they said. I stepped out onto what was left of the porch, holding the rifle steady in both hands.

I looked out over the lake again. The mist was rising more quickly now, and hints of sunlight glinted through rifts in the clouds. The canoe was closer, and I saw a man sitting in the stern, a big man judging from how low the canoe sat in the water. He moved his paddle with swift and powerful strokes. He was making good speed, and as he got closer, his features and clothing became gradually more distinct.

He was broad shouldered with heavily muscled arms and big hands. His face was somewhat obscured by a wide brim hat, but I could see that he had a full beard and thick reddish hair that fell over the collar of his shirt.

I heard the steady sound of his paddle now as it lifted in and out of the water. Once he raised his head and stared in the direction of the cabin, searching. I shrank back against the door, out of sight. He had not seen me. I waited, uncertainly, for his arrival.

When he reached the shore, the man stepped clumsily onto the partially submerged remains of the landing and began walking up the hill toward me. He moved slowly, picking his way up the gully, which had been the path. In his right hand, he carried a double-bitted ax.

He stopped several yards away from the cabin, and I watched warily as he took in the scene around him. There was something familiar about him, but I was not sure. Finally, his eyes turned towards the ruined porch and he saw me standing there, with the rifle in my hands, staring at him. He started slightly, seeming unsure what to do next.

For a moment, neither of us spoke, appraising each other. I could see his face clearly now as he stood looking at me. It was wide and deeply colored by the sun, open and strong. His mouth, surrounded by the curling red hair of his beard, was soft and full.

"Mornin', Mrs. Benson," he called out, at last, touching the brim of his hat. "My name is Ben Stone. I hope I did not frighten you?" (He said it as a question, not a statement.) "Your Aunt Rebecca sent me to see if you are all right. With the storm and all, she was worried about you being stranded out here all alone with the little ones." His voice was deep and had an accent that reminded me of the French-Canadian children who had come to our school so long ago. He paused for a moment, waiting for a response.

I said nothing, not sure what was expected of me. He went on, "The bridge is washed out and your road in is impassable—I had to come by canoe. The whole county has been hit pretty hard." He paused again, shifting his weight, and looking at his hands. "I came to see if you needed any assistance." I began to feel myself relax a little. A heavy weight was slowly lifting off my chest.

"I suppose we could be using some extra hands," I said, looking at the chaos surrounding us. I felt the rifle still heavy in my hands and smiled apologetically. "We do not get many visitors out here," I said, as I propped the gun against the house. I could almost feel Ben let out a long breath.

The door behind me opened a crack, and Sarah and Jacob peeked out. "Come, children, and meet our new friend, Mr. Stone." I gathered them in my arms and held them a moment while they looked shyly at Ben. He stood awkwardly, hat in hand, smiling back at them. Sunny sniffed cautiously around his legs and feet. Ben reached out a hand gently for Sunny to smell.

It came to me, then, where I had seen Ben before. It was at a church social that my aunt had forced me to go to last winter. Ben had stood at the back of the room, looking as uncomfortable and out of place in his Sunday best, as I felt. I had pleaded a headache and gone home early.

Suddenly I began to laugh, my first real laugh in many months. It felt good.

"Well," I chuckled when I could finally catch my breath. "It sure looks as if Aunt Rebecca finally got her way!"

Ben looked at me quizzically.

"My aunt has been trying to introduce me to a nice, hardworking young man for months, now," I said, still chuckling. "She would be horrified at the reception I have given you!"

I looked down at my soiled dress and tried ineffectually to arrange my disheveled hair. "I must look a fright," I said, without embarrassment. "The children can show you around while I clean up and then we can have some breakfast. We have a lot of work to do, Mr. Ben Stone!"

As Jacob and Sarah led Ben toward the barn, all puffed with pride, given the responsibility of guides, I entered the house. On my way through the center room towards my bedroom to change out of my wet and ruined dress, something made me look into the far corner. There stood my sewing machine, neglected and untouched under dusty blankets these many months.

"A quilt," I said to myself. "I will make a new quilt to mark a new beginning." An image of a quilt I had admired made by my aunt some years before came to my mind. What was the name of that pattern? I pondered a moment. North Wind, I think, a variation of the Birds in the Air quilt I made as a young girl.

"I will make mine of brighter colors, with lots of reds and yellows, with greens, browns, and blues for earth and sky. Perhaps I will even appliqué flowers all around the border. I shall call my quilt 'After the Storm'." I smiled with satisfaction and moved with a lighter step towards my bedroom.

Journal Entry, August 1885

Dearest Mama – Another calamity has befallen us, this time in the form of a great storm. I have never in my life experienced such winds and rain that fell upon our little cabin in the woods. It was as if the entire wrath of nature fell upon us. It destroyed much of our property and caused great damage across the entire region, including the village. I heard that the wind tore roofs off houses and barns and many trees came down. Our road is impassable so I have not yet ventured into town to see what I can do to help. I thank the good Lord that the worst is over now. A truly kind man, Mr. Ben Stone, has arrived from town (sent by Aunt Rebecca, as you might guess), to see what he can do to help us. In spite of all, I am feeling hopeful that perhaps this great storm has blown away the last of these past two bitter years and I can finally start a new chapter in my life. Please say a prayer to help sustain us through the coming weeks and months of rebuilding and repairs.

Your grateful daughter, Hannah

CARY FLANAGAN

Chapter Twenty-Seven

In the weeks that followed the storm, Ben came to the cabin to help me almost every day along with Will and sometimes Jesse or Daniel. Lizzy came too when she was not needed at home. They traveled by canoe until they were able to clear the road enough to use. Jesse said that they had lost quite a few of the apple trees toward the top of the hill where they were exposed, and the storm severely damaged their barn as well. Daniel said many trees were lost along the lakeshore and in town but, fortunately, their inn survived with only minor damage. He and his brothers were dividing their time between helping me and their own families.

We cut and burned broken tree limbs and smashed boards in bonfires over my vegetable garden. We also cleaned and piled up bricks from the chimney before rebuilding it. The barn would need a new roof—so many things to do! I wondered, some days, if we could ever finish such a daunting task!

At one point, in an attempt to bring some humor to the situation, Will quipped, "Well, at least with all these trees down you have a great start on clearing the land for new pastures and you have a lifetime supply of firewood!"

Ben worked hard alongside Aaron's brothers, cutting up the sprawl of downed trees while I tended the bonfires or worked on gathering anything that needed burning. The children helped as best they could, gathering twigs, pinecones, and small pieces of wood for the bonfire. Lizzy prepared a generous lunch for all of us when she was there. I was grateful beyond measure for their help and support.

I liked Ben right away. He was a breath of fresh air after so many dark months, and I began to dare hope that better things might lie ahead of me. Ben had an easygoing and gentle nature but did not hesitate to throw himself completely into salvaging what we could, and rebuilding what was lost. I did not think of him in a romantic way for many months after we first met but he impressed me with his thoughtfulness and his willingness to work hard. The way he treated Jacob and Sarah was a wonder. They came to adore him, especially Jacob. I was also amused to find that Sunny began to shadow his every step.

In the quiet moments of the evening, after the men left and I had tucked the children in for the night, I began to ponder what it might be like to make room in my life and my heart for a new man. The thought scared me, but it would not leave me alone. It kept tapping me on the shoulder and nagging at me when I tried to push it away. Would it be disloyal to Aaron? Would it mean I no longer loved him? Would it even be possible for me to fall in love with someone else? Such thoughts whirled around in my mind when I was trying to fall asleep.

It was not long before I noticed that Will and Ben were in some kind of competition with each other. Each one tried to outdo the other in the amount of wood he could carry or the number of bricks he arranged in neat piles. In the beginning, I thought it was a game for them, and I remember teasing them about it once. Then I realized they were serious.

I confess I did not understand the motive behind this game at first, but it warmed my heart to think that two men that I cared about seemed to be vying for my attention. It embarrasses me now to think how blind I was then! Will admitted to me years later that he would have courted me in earnest if he had thought he had a chance. However, he saw the way Ben looked at me and how this contest was going to go long before I had any inkling there was a contest. Will began making excuses for why he did not come as often and I found, to my surprise, that I missed him when he was not there.

I began watching Ben out of the corner of my eye when I did not think he noticed and continued my ponderings alone in my bed at night. What if?

I sometimes wondered how different my life would have been if Aaron had not been taken from me. We would have, I am sure, continued to live a quiet but fulfilling life with only a very modest income. More children would have been born to us and we would have been happy all our days together. Sadly, that was not God's plan, and I did not dwell on that thought very much.

Aaron and Ben were so different in some ways yet much the same in others. Aaron was not tall—we were of a height, him, and me. He had thick black hair and kept his face well shaven. He was wiry and strong and had boundless energy always with a smile on his face. He loved to tease and have fun. He was more outgoing than I was and loved the social gatherings we attended a few times a year. He adored the children and me as we adored him. So many sweet memories.

Ben was a big man, tall and muscular, with soft curly red hair and a full beard. He was of French-Canadian stock, I learned later, although one grandfather came over to Canada from Ireland during the famine years. That must have been where his red hair came from.

Ben told me once that he was the youngest of eight in a Quebecois' farming family with no prospects of inheriting any land and that his father beat him. He left home at seventeen and changed his name so no one could trace him. His story was similar to that of my twin uncles who ran away from their abusive father to go west. I admired his courage to leave home and forge a new life for himself but felt sorry for his mother.

Ben was remarkably strong and sometimes reminded me of a great bear. He was self-confident and steady and could work for hours. He was also gentle and shy and smiled often, his eyes twinkling. To my surprise, I learned he was a great storyteller— Jacob and Sarah would hang on his arms sometimes and beg him for a story.

Tired as he was after a day's work, we would sit in a circle with him by the fire as he told his tales before he went home. He told stories of the great north woods, and of the farm he left when he was seventeen. Stories of old Ireland that he had heard his Gran' Da tell. Some of his stories were from the lumber camps that he worked in when he was a young man, but many of those were not fit for children's ears.

Ben had a way of making almost any story amusing and the children rewarded him with gales of laughter. He even made me laugh, sometimes. I gradually came to appreciate the fine man he was and looked forward to his arrival each day.

After many weeks, the repairs to the barn were almost finished, new fences had been built, the chimneys stood tall again above the cabin, and my gardens were ready for spring.

One evening, after the children were in bed, Ben lingered after the others had left. I sensed he had something on his mind as he stood nervously near the door. Finally, he asked me, shyly:

"Do you think you would ever consider marrying again?"

I said, quite honestly, "I don't know."

He told me, then, all in a rush, what was in his heart. "I care deeply for you, Hannah. You amaze me with your strength and your courage. You are a wonder to me. Your children—I love them, too, as if they were my own. I hope I am not speaking out of turn—this may be too soon for you to hear, but I want to be part of your life, Hannah, for always." He cupped my face in his hands and spoke softly. "I know this has been an exceedingly difficult time for you, Hannah, I but want to court you when you are ready. I hope you will consider what I am saying."

Before I knew what I was doing, my arms were around his neck. I whispered into his ear, "I am ready!"

After that, we held hands in the early evening and talked after the others had left. I was surprised to find that I felt the old yearning ache in me again and was sad when Ben left to go home.

One night, as he was getting ready to leave, I decided to take matters into my own hands. We were standing close together but not touching and I suddenly rose on my tiptoes and kissed his cheek. (I was surprised by how soft his beard was, soft as a baby's hair. I had expected it to be wiry and rough.)

As I stood leaning lightly against him, I whispered, "Do you really have to go? Would you like to stay here with me tonight?" He put his arms around my shoulders and gently kissed the top of my head. "It would be best to wait until the preacher has us say our 'I do's. But know this, my darling, every night until then I will dream of you lying in my arms."

Journal Entry, November 1885

Dearest Mama – A wondrous thing has happened! Ben has asked me to marry him, and I said yes! Oh, Mama, I never thought I would be able to love again but Ben is so kind and so thoughtful and he loves my children as if they were his own. I will never stop loving Aaron and I know Ben understands that, but Ben has been stealing his way into my heart for many months without me even realizing it until now. Is it possible to be so happy twice in a lifetime?

Your incredibly happy daughter, Hannah

Chapter Twenty-Eight

In August 1886, Ben and I were married in the same church as Aaron and I had been married in what seemed like another lifetime. I felt moved beyond words when almost the entire Benson family came to witness the marriage and to wish us both well. Only Will was missing.

Having no one to "give me away," Mr. Benson offered his arm once again. I struggled to maintain my composure as he handed me to Ben. "You are doing the right thing," he whispered in my ear as he kissed my cheek. "Aaron would have wanted it this way. Blessings upon you and Ben, and may this marriage be as happy and fruitful as your first."

Aunt Rebecca had made me a beautiful dress of soft green with white lace and many ruffles and flounces, and with a matching cap and veil. Lydia had helped me dress my hair with fresh flowers from my aunt's garden—white roses and baby's breath—and I carried a bouquet of the same flowers. Sarah led the procession, spreading rose petals before me and my handsome son, Jacob, bore the ring on a velvet pillow. At the altar, Lydia and Jane stood on one side while

Ben, smiling shyly, waited for me to take his hand.

After the service and the festivities, Ben surprised me with a trip to North Conway in a rented buggy to one of the new grand hotels. Ben had apprenticed with a master builder in Conway and did some of the finish work on this hotel. Our stay there was a wedding gift from his mentor, Mr. Blakeley. The generosity of this gift overwhelmed me, as well as the grandeur of the hotel, the elegance of the rooms, and the sumptuous food.

I was also dizzy and nervous as I anticipated our first night together as husband and wife. Ben felt my nervousness and was very thoughtful and gentle, not wanting to rush me. I admit it was a bit awkward, at first. Somehow, I felt I was being disloyal to Aaron, but Ben was tender and patient with me. I had not realized until then how much I had missed the touch of a man's hands on my body, how much I had ached with loneliness and need. As we melted together in the darkness, I was filled with joy and knew I could be whole once again.

When we returned from our honeymoon, Ben moved out to the farm to live with my children and me. It was wonderful that he no longer had to leave to go home at the end of each day. I cherished the heat of his hands on me as he held me close at night, and my heart sang at the tenderness with which he touched my hand or brushed the back of my neck with a kiss during the day when Jacob and Sarah were not watching. I loved how Ben played games with them and let them "help" him when he tended to the animals and did his other chores, and he was still a great storyteller. Ben's favorite story, which he never seemed to tire of, was the time when he first met me.

"Your mother had a shotgun in her hands, and she clearly knew how to use it!" he would say. "I didn't know if I was about to be welcomed or blown to pieces!" Then he would roar with laughter.

It was a wonder how quickly Ben became a seamless part of our family. It seemed we were all drunk with love!

We eventually settled into a rhythm dictated by the seasons. In late fall, we moved from the farm to Ben's home in Conway where we spent the winters until we could return in the spring to the farm. It was quite a sight when we packed up all the family belongings along with Sunny and the children in one wagon with the chickens, goats, and enough provisions to last us through the warm months in another and then reversed the process in the fall.

When Rebecca Caroline was born a year after we married, Ben was besotted with her. She had the prettiest eyes, he said, and he had never seen such blonde curls on a baby and on and on! He could not get enough of her little fingers and toes, and her gurgles and chortles made him laugh aloud! I loved watching the two of them together. Ben enjoyed carrying little Becky around on his shoulders or bouncing her on his knees playing horsey. She giggled so loudly that everyone within earshot giggled too, just to hear her.

Lydia Jane came next in 1890. She was a tiny little thing with dark red hair like her father. We named her for my two closest friends, Lydia, and Jane but called her Lyddie. I worried a bit at first because she was so small, but she began to gain weight and soon caught up to Becky in size. Becky was not at all sure what to make of this interloper, but nine-year-old Sarah played with her and made sure she got plenty of attention when I was nursing the baby.

In 1892, Benjamin Thomas arrived. He was a big strapping boy and looked as if he would be tall like his father, whose name he shared. We called him Benny. My how fast he grew! Jacob was wonderful with him, especially once he learned to walk. After that, Benny became Jacob's shadow, following him around the house like a puppy dog when Jacob was not in school.

Margaret Abigail followed a few years later, in 1895. She had my blond hair and was a happy child who rarely fussed. Sarah turned fourteen that year and was a big help with the new baby, whom we called Maggie, and the other children. However, I also noticed she seemed distant and sullen at times. I regret I was too busy to take much notice and did not attempt to find out what was troubling her.

Ben loved them all and was a wonderful father to each, but I think Becky was always his favorite because she was his first.

As each baby arrived, I sewed beautiful little outfits, quilts, and all the other things an infant and young child need. Of course, Jacob and Sarah had outgrown all the things I made for them and the new little ones received some of those "hand-me-downs."

I made new clothes for Jacob who was growing like a weed and for Sarah. Goodness, how fast children outgrow what you make for them to wear!

Our little family went to church in the village on Sundays and then spent the afternoon visiting with my aunt and Lydia. Sometimes Rose and Daniel came, or Jane and her husband, or Lydia's good friend Lucy Hastings. I also attended our quilting bee as often as I could. I was so much busier now with a new pregnancy every couple of years and active toddlers to look after. Thankfully, Jacob and Sarah were a big help with the chores and Sarah was wonderful with the babies, most of the time. Sometimes I even caught a short nap in the afternoons while she looked after them.

I continued to make quilts when I had time, usually sewing in the evenings when I finished my chores for the day and the children were in bed. I was often exhausted by that time and the light from the kerosene lamps was hard on my eyes so I could not get a lot done. It was frustrating at times, but my children, whom I loved with a fierce passion, took so much of my attention that I did not mind so much. I wanted to capture every moment while they were still little and needed me.

We spent part of every summer at the small farm by the lake though with our large family and Ben's growing building business, it was hard to spend as many weeks there as we had before. We added a sleeping porch to one side of the house, which helped, and Ben often spent a few days in town, visiting us on the weekends. I missed spending as much time there as in the past but did not really mind. I had so much on my plate in those days it was easier to stay in town.

Still, I looked forward to seeing the lake and enjoying the quiet (though not so quiet with young children playing everywhere, and the dog barking along with their shrieks of laughter.)

We taught the children to swim and paddle a canoe, which they loved, with either Ben or Jacob keeping careful watch. Ben took Jacob and one or another of the children fishing whenever he came out to the farm for a few days, rewarding us with delicious dinners of fresh trout.

With everyone's help, Ben built a large wooden dock and a separate float one summer and the children never seemed to tire of jumping off one or the other into the water. They loved having Sunny with them again as well. It was great fun tossing sticks for him, and he enjoyed jumping into the water with the children. (A house in town is no place for an active working dog, so he lived most of the time with his canine friends at the Benson farm.)

Sadly, after a good long life, Sunny left us in the summer before Maggie was born. We had been staying at the farm and had brought him with us from the Benson farm as usual. I noticed he was much thinner and had less energy than before.

When we first arrived, Sunny tried to explore all his favorite places around the cabin and barn but without the same eagerness. I watched with great sadness as he eventually stopped eating and finally failed altogether. The children and I sat with him on the grass near the garden, and I held him as he slipped away. Each of us cried as we buried him in the place he had loved so much. It was a sad day.

Chapter Twenty-Nine

Ben had created a successful business over the years as a builder and cabinetmaker. He worked on the growing numbers of grand hotels that were going up in the White Mountains. For the first time in my life, I did not feel I needed to pinch every penny. It felt strange at first, but I liked it!

After the railroad came through the center of our village in 1870, folks from Boston and New York started coming to our part of the state to spend the summer in the fresh mountain air. Others came and stayed. Not long after the new railroad station was completed, a Mr. Greenough, a lumber operator, and investor, built a beautiful inn right on the shores of Easton Lake. Ben did most of the finish work on the rooms that overlooked the water. He worked on many such projects as a master builder, and I marveled at how different my life was from the poverty of my early childhood.

Life in our little village changed as more families moved to the area. More stores opened and several small guesthouses and cottages appeared on the shores of the lake. The summer visitors who arrived every spring or early summer added much to the summer festivities. It was fun to see the wealthy people from Boston or New York arrive at the station with their fancy baggage and servants. Every hotel and small inn had carriages and wagons waiting at the station to fetch the new arrivals to their appointed destination.

My aunt, with Lydia's assistance, was still making dresses to order, and she began to cater to the expensive tastes of the summer tourists. The wealthy visitors liked to have everything custom made for them and they provided a steady source of income. My aunt even purchased the latest model of Singer treadle sewing machine so that she and Lydia could both sew at the same time. It seemed like almost everyone prospered as our little village grew into a real town.

It was not long before Ben's house in Conway became too small for us. We were busting at the seams by the time Maggie arrived in the winter of 1895. The previous fall, Ben began building a large ornate house on the main street of our village with plenty of room for our growing family. It was near the railroad station and had lovely views of the lake from the graceful veranda that framed the front and sides and from every front-facing upstairs window.

It was the largest home I had ever seen! There were three floors and seven bedrooms. Each of our children had their own room, an unheard-of luxury. There were two indoor bathrooms and a playroom for the children on the top floor. From my humble beginnings, it was difficult to fathom such grandeur!

Every week after church, while the house was under construction, Ben took the children and me over to the building site and showed us how it was progressing. It was marvelous, all the fine workmanship and modern conveniences. Can you imagine? Not just one indoor bathroom, but two, and both cold and hot running water in the kitchen! I was thrilled to see the house move toward completion and was so proud of Ben. I marveled at his vision and his skills as a builder.

When we were finally able to move in, Ben sold his house in Conway and used the money to build a large barn behind the house. He set up a workshop in the shed that connected the house with the barn where he kept his woodworking tools and did most of his finish work.

As you can imagine, moving day was quite an event! Six children (including new baby Maggie, born just before we left the old house) and our furnishings, coming all the way from Conway to our new home— more than fifteen miles by horse-drawn wagons. The older children were immensely helpful, especially Jacob, who was nearly grown at eighteen. Sarah did a good job keeping the little ones organized and mostly under control. She was fifteen and quite capable, but she did not have Jacob's maturity, and the little ones at ages eight, five, three and newborn, were quite a handful! I asked Lydia to come and help Sarah and me with the children once we arrived. Thankfully, Ben hired some men to help with the heavy work of loading and unloading.

When we completed the barn later that year, it included comfortable stalls for Molly (who had become too old for doing much work by then) and for the carriage horses and goats, that we kept. Attached to the back of the shed was a chicken coop for our twelve laying hens and a rooster.

When one of Aunt Rebecca's cats had kittens, I allowed the children, after much cajoling, to pick out two kittens to bring home when they were old enough. I had forgotten how cute and playful kittens could be. Their antics entranced the children, and they were constantly chasing after them. As the kittens grew older, the mouse population in the house and barn dwindled, which I noted with great satisfaction.

Ben took on Jesse Benson as an apprentice when there was more work than he could handle by himself. The two of them made a great team. I enjoyed seeing Jesse when he came down from the farm and it felt good to renew a connection with one of Aaron's closest brothers.

Chapter Thirty

One of the first things Ben did when we moved into the new house was to hire a housekeeper/nanny and a cook. Oh my, what a luxury! At first, I rebelled against this idea as too extravagant. However, I was grateful once I got used to the notion that I no longer had to do everything myself. With a house full of children, it made an enormous difference in my life.

For the first time since I could remember, I could sew during the day while the children were in school or minded by Gladys, our young redheaded Irish girl. She was wonderful with the children and they adored her. She played games with them, told stories about her life in Ireland, took them out for walks, and generally kept them happy and entertained. In addition, she kept the house tidy and clean. She was a treasure!

Then there was Sallie Mae, our new cook, and my quilting assistant. She was Clara Foster's daughter, whom I had first met years ago when I was only seventeen or eighteen. She was four when her family arrived from the south after the war. Now she had grown into an attractive and bright young woman. Her mother had taught her how to manage a kitchen and she had learned to sew and make quilts with remarkable skill. I invited her to join our quilting bee when she was old enough, just as I had invited her mother before her and now, she had joined our family.

Sallie Mae was always cheerful and full of energy. I enjoyed talking with her every day while we planned menus, shopping lists, or quilting projects I might need help with. I looked forward to mealtimes after she came to us, both for her delicious cooking and for the fact that I no longer had to prepare the meal or clean up after it! We were so lucky to have her there. Gladys and Sallie Mae were both real gifts to our family and I will be forever grateful to each of them for allowing me to get some of my life back.

It seemed as if we were finally on a smooth path except for Sarah. As she grew older, she became more headstrong and defiant, and her dark moods more frequent. She was not happy living in town and seemed happiest only at our little farm in the summer. She was angry or depressed by turns. I did not know how to help her, and I felt in my heart that it would not be long before she flew away from us.

Journal Entry Fall 1896

Dearest Mama— Ben and I are truly blessed. We now have four beautiful children together and I swear he loves each one more than the last! Jacob, at eighteen, is of age now, and Sarah, at 15, has entered that difficult age between childhood and adulthood. She is wonderful with the children and seems to be happy for a while. Then her mood darkens. She becomes angry and sullen over small things. If I ask her what is bothering her, she just turns away and says I would not understand. I fear for her and wish I had someone to advise me as to how to talk to her about this. To his great credit, Ben has always paid particular attention to Jacob and Sarah lest they feel slighted. Lately, he has been teaching Jacob some of the basics of wood joinery and cabinet making. I love seeing Jacob work alongside Ben and his uncle Jesse. It amazes me how much Jacob looks like both his father and his uncle. I am so proud of him. With Sarah, I am holding my breath and keeping my fingers crossed that she could overcome the darkness she holds inside herself. It hurts me to see her this way.

Your loving daughter, Hannah

One afternoon when we had been in the new house for about six months, Sarah came tiptoeing into my sewing room and asked if she could talk to me. She said she had some questions.

"Of course, dear," I said, setting aside the quilt I was working on and moving some fabric off the other chair so she could sit. Sarah looked nervous, but took a big breath and said, "

You know I love Ben, don't you?" I nodded, afraid to say something that might spoil the moment. "I do love him, Mama, but he is not my father. I feel like I have a huge empty place inside of me where my father should be. I do not know how to fill the emptiness. I know Ben loves me too, but I cannot help feeling as if I had to give way to his children ever since you and he got married. I don't feel like I belong." She burst into tears and I put my arms around her.

"Oh, dearest one, of course, you belong! We both love you, just as we love Jacob and the little ones. They have not replaced you. Please believe me when I say I know what it feels like to lose a parent. I do. I lost both of mine around the same age you lost your father. For many years, I had the same empty place inside of me that you describe."

Sarah said nothing and I took a deep breath.

"Your father was a good man and my dearest friend, Sarah. He was a wonderful husband and loving father to you and Jacob. If I could have held onto him forever, I would have wanted nothing more. However, it did not happen that way. Sometimes an event can turn your life upside down in an instant and nothing is ever the same again. That is just the way life can be."

Wiping her eyes, Sara looked at me and asked, "Did you love my father as much as you love Ben? Did you love one more than the other?" I could hear the edge in her voice.

"Sarah, your father was my first and dearest love. You need to believe that and, as I have said, I never wanted anything else in my life but him and the children we would have raised together. I did not have that choice. All I can say is that the two men were different, and we shared different things. But the love I felt for each of them was and is deep and real."

I took another breath, gathering my thoughts. "Your father and I grew up together from childhood. We were best friends long before we ever fell in love and married. I met Ben when I was almost 30 under difficult circumstances. I liked him immediately, and grew to appreciate his many fine qualities, but it was not until many months after we first met that I began to care about him as more than a friend. I feel very blessed to have found Ben when I did. There was a time before I met him that I was not sure I would be able to survive the loss of your father.

"Please, do not ever doubt how much Ben loves you. He fell in love with you and Jacob long before he fell in love with me." Sarah said nothing.

"Do you believe what I am telling you, Sarah?"

"Yes," she said, in a small voice. "Don't tell Ben we talked about this, Mama. Promise me."

"I promise," I said, and kissed her cheek. "I love you."

"I love you too" she whispered and left the room.

I went back to my sewing after Sarah left, feeling as if an enormous weight was lifting off my shoulders. We had finally connected, and I was grateful she had found the courage to talk about the pain she had been carrying around all these years.

...

Journal Entry, December 1896

Dearest Mama— Ben continues to surprise me every day. For Christmas this year, he presented the children with a wondrous gift. He had built a three-foot tall dollhouse, which is an exact replica of the house we are living in! Every detail is there, right down to the shingles on the roof and the fancy turned spindles on the verandah railing. He even painted the outside to match the pale yellow of our own house, complete with white trim. In addition, he made tiny pieces of furniture for the different rooms. The front of the house and the roof come off to see inside and to move things around. You should have seen the children's eyes when they first saw it! I was deeply touched. The children are enchanted, except, of course, Benny, but I think he understands what a special gift this is. Even Sarah was impressed. Ben has apparently been working in secret for many months to complete this house in time for Christmas. It now sits in a place of honor in our parlor and the girls have been having a lovely time making up stories about who lives there.

Your happy daughter, Hannah

Chapter Thirty-One

1897

I spent many happy hours sewing and making quilts with the extra help Gladys and Sallie Mae gave me. I relished being able to work uninterrupted for several hours almost every day while the children napped or were in school. What bliss!

I began to experiment with new quilt designs. I would get an idea for a block and graph it out on paper then choose my colors and make the block. Now that I did not have to rely only on scraps of fabric, I made my quilts any color I wanted. What fun it was to be able to go to the general store and pick out fabrics and threads for my next project. Jane was always happy to help me make my choices and cut a very generous yard of fabric for me when her mother was not looking. (Jane and her husband Sam were running the store by now with a greatly expanded inventory. Her parents helped a few hours per day, enjoying some much-deserved leisure time, after all their years of hard work.)

I continued to go to our quilting bee every month at Aunt Rebecca's house. Rebecca was still active in the group in spite of her more than seventy years. Each month, when I attended bee, I brought some of my new ideas and sample blocks or quilts to see what the others thought of them. Usually, the other quilters liked what they saw and wanted to make a quilt like mine. They began asking me to write up the directions and teach them how to make that design. Of course, I said yes! I enjoyed seeing how the quilts that my friends made from my patterns turned out using their own color choices.

An idea began forming in my mind after the members of my bee used several of my designs. Could I find a way to write up directions and draft blocks so that any quilter who wanted could purchase them and make a quilt for herself? I had never heard of anyone doing that before in the area where I lived but I decided "Why Not?"

The first step, I thought, was to consult with Mr. Ramsey who published a weekly newspaper for our village and the surrounding towns. His office was not far from where I lived so I went to see him one day, pushing baby Maggie in her wicker carriage. When I explained my errand, Mr. Ramsey was most kind and he offered, for a small fee, to put one of my quilt designs into the next issue of his paper. He set the type for my directions himself and created an image of my block design, as an illustration, to go with them. I almost held my breath for a week to see what would happen when the paper came out.

Only a few establishments at that time had a telephone. Mr. Ramsey's printing and newspaper office was one of them. After the first issue came out with my quilt design in it, a few people called him to say what a wonderful idea it was to include this new quilt pattern and wondering if there would be more. Mr. Ramsey agreed to run another design the following week. I cannot tell you how thrilled I was.

Soon, readership of Mr. Ramsey's paper increased, and I no longer had to pay him to include my patterns. Then I thought what if I had him typeset my patterns and print them in a size and format that could be packaged and mailed. We tried that idea, and my little mail order quilt pattern business was born!

I had six new pattern designs ready by that time and my older children helped me pack the patterns as people asked for them. Mr. Ramsey charged me $.08 per copy to print the patterns and I sold them for $.28 each plus a penny for postage. I was making a profit!

In the fall of 1897, I decided I needed to spread my wings, and search out a wider readership. I contacted newspaper publishers in larger cities such as Manchester, New Hampshire and Boston, Massachusetts. I also contacted the publishers of several magazines that catered to women. I placed small ads with diagrams of my quilt designs, and to my enormous surprise, orders for my patterns started coming in—slowly at first, then in a steady stream. I was beyond pleased and I think Ben was proud of my new enterprise as well.

We developed a little home industry with the older children folding the printed patterns and packaging them. I looked forward to seeing what orders arrived for me at the post office. Gladys and I walked to the school every afternoon with baby Maggie in her pram and Benny walking beside us. We would collect the older children and then I would go on to the post office with the baby to check out our mailbox and to drop off the orders from the day before while Gladys walked home with the other children. Occasionally, all the children wanted to come with me, and we formed a little procession, walking in great anticipation along the main street to the post office.

My success felt strange to me—I knew we did not need the income but somehow, the extra money that came in as a direct result of my efforts made all the difference in how I felt about myself. It is hard to explain—I know in modern times women often contribute significantly to family income but in those days, it was a rarity. I began to feel as if I was somebody, not just a wife and mother.

I tried to keep those feelings to myself, remembering from earliest childhood not to act proud or to put on airs. Nonetheless, I could not help feeling pleased with my accomplishments, especially when people I met told me how wonderful my quilts and my patterns were and how talented they thought I was. Occasionally, I received notes from people who had ordered one or more patterns in which they said much the same. How could I not feel proud of what I was doing?

Journal Entry, August 1897

Dearest Mama – You will never believe this: I received a gracious letter of inquiry today from the Editor of the Ladies' Home journal. They want to come and interview me and take photos of my quilts and write a story about ME! I accepted their offer right away. As you can imagine I feel like I am floating three feet off the ground right now. My family and friends are as thrilled as I am and have decided this is cause for a great celebration as it is only a few days before my fortieth birthday. Ben decreed we should host a grand party to honor both accomplishments. What a dear man. I am so blessed!

Your delighted daughter, Hannah

The day the photographer, Mr. Jenkins, and journalist, Mr. Sandhurst arrived there was big excitement in our household. I made sure all the children scrubbed themselves clean and wore their Sunday best (after all, they were my "business associates").

The only person missing was Sarah—no one seemed to know where she was. I was disappointed she would not be included in the photograph. I also asked Aunt Rebecca to come, and Lydia, Jane, and Rose, and all the members of our quilting bee, including Clara and Sallie Mae, since they were each such an important part of my development as a quilter. I even asked Ben to carry out my treasured sewing machine, a real "antique" by now! Friends and neighbors stood nearby to watch what was happening. I guess we made quite a spectacle of ourselves!

More than a dozen of my quilts hung outside on lines or lay over chairs and sofas to make them easier to photograph in the natural outdoor light, along with several made by members of our bee from my patterns. As I told my story to the journalist, I was nervous at first, feeling tongue-tied and embarrassed, but soon felt more comfortable. I told him how I learned to quilt, about our quilting bee, how I experimented with designing my own patterns, and then found a way to market them. Mr. Sandhurst asked many questions, and he was good about including the children. Mr. Jenkins took many photographs of our entire family, our bee members, and some of me standing with Ben, holding three-year-old Maggie. Then he took a photo of me sitting at my treadle machine, pretending to teach eleven-year-old Becky how to sew. Oh my, I felt my head swell up with pride! The two gentlemen were very gracious.

"Thank you so much, Mrs. Stone. Your quilts are wonderful and the information you gave us will make a splendid article!" He promised to send me several free copies of the magazine and a gift certificate for a subscription when the article appeared in print.

"I am sure lots of business will come your way as a result of this article," he said, as he and Mr. Jenkins took their leave. That evening, we celebrated our big adventure and my success with a potluck dinner for all our friends and neighbors. I received lots of congratulations and well wishes, and Ben gave me a big hug in front of everybody and told me how proud he was of my accomplishments! I was fairly flying and felt like a celebrity!

About six months later, we had a second celebration after we received our copies of the Ladies Home Journal. Right there, on the cover, was a photograph of me with all the members of our bee and several of my quilts displayed in front of the group. Ben began to tease me, saying that my head was growing too big for my hats!

Journal Entry February 1898

Dearest Mama - I am famous! Can you imagine it? Who would have ever thought a girl from a small village in New Hampshire could be famous for designing quilts! I have received letters and orders for patterns from many parts of this country. I hope you are proud of me, Mama. I wish you and Papa could both be here to witness my success!

I will be forever grateful to Aunt Rebecca for teaching me to sew and for nurturing my dream as it has developed, and Ben, as well. I do not know many husbands who would tolerate, let alone support a recognized businessperson for a wife. Even the children are excited. They have been telling their friends and schoolmates about their famous mother!

I am also grateful to the members of my bee and applaud them. They have been encouraging me for many years and have "tested out" my patterns. They, too, are pleased that the magazine article mentioned them by name. This has been a genuinely great experience for all of us.

Your happy and appreciative daughter, Hannah

Chapter Thirty-Two

Why is it that when things are going well in one's life, something happens to change everything? A few days after the second celebration of my big success, an elderly man knocked on our front door, asking to see Miss Lydia and Miss Rose Murray. Gladys answered the door and told him Miss Lydia and Miss Rose did not live at this address. I heard their voices and Lydia's name and came to see who was there.

The man had long gray hair that was uncombed and dirty with a scraggly gray beard. He was dressed in shabby clothes and held a worn hat in his hands. At first, I thought he might be a beggar asking for assistance.

"Can we help you, sir? If you need a good meal, please come around to the back where the kitchen is. My cook will gladly make you a plate."

"No ma'am," he said. "My name is Joseph Murray. I am looking for my two daughters, Lydia, and Rose, who were taken away from me many years ago."

I struggled not to let the shock show on my face.

"Well, Mr. Murray, it is nice to see you again," I said, my voice a bit unsteady. "Gladys, would you be so kind as to fetch Mr. Stone right away and tell him we have a visitor? And ask Sallie Mae to bring us a pot of tea and some sandwiches." Gladys looked uncertainly from me to Mr. Murray then quickly left the room.

"How did you happen to come here, Mr. Murray? And why now, after all these years?" I asked, stepping away from him. A strong odor came from his unwashed body and soiled clothes.

Mr. Murray shook his head, said only that he had been "detained" for some years, and could not come until now. "A few days ago, I saw a magazine on a newsstand which had a photograph on the front cover of a whole group of ladies and some quilts." He held out a crumpled sheet of paper and I recognized the photograph immediately. Mr. Murray continued,

"I looked at the picture more carefully and saw you, ma'am and a woman who looked a lot like my Lydia, even after all these years not seeing her. I did not recognize this house, but I remembered you—you and Lydia being such good friends and all when I last saw you. I decided to come here and see if it was her in the photo and to look for my other daughter, Rose. Do you know where I can find them?"

"No," I lied. (May the good Lord forgive me.) "Rose is married, and Lydia has moved away. But I can ask around to see if anyone in the town might know." I was stalling, hoping Ben would appear soon.

Mr. Murray still stood in the doorway. He looked agitated and upset. "Where are my girls? I have come such a long way to find them. They are all I have left in this wretched world." Tears began to course down his grimy cheeks.

Just then, Sallie Mae brought in the tea. Ben and Jacob came in right behind her, followed a few minutes later by Jesse and the sheriff. I saw each of them take in the situation. Ben held out his hand to the man at the door.

"Mr. Murray, I am Ben Stone, these folks here are my wife, Hannah, my friend Jesse and my son Jacob." (I saw a flicker of surprise and pleasure in Jacob's eyes.) "And this here is another good friend, Mr. Jamison, sheriff of this village. You are welcome to join us for tea while we discuss your concerns."

"I ain't got no concerns. I just want to know where my girls are and have a chance to talk to them, and then I will be on my way."

The sheriff spoke.

"I am afraid we can't do that, Mr. Murray, until we have a better idea of your intentions and plans." Everyone was quiet, waiting.

Mr. Murray spoke again, spitting out the words. "What right do you have to keep a man away from his own children?" His eyes began to fill again, and he turned his head away.

"Mr. Murray," Ben said calmly, "Lydia and Rose are both grown women now, with lives of their own. They are free to make their own decisions. Rose has a husband and children. Lydia has a whole 'family' of friends, including us, who will stand by her. Perhaps we can arrange for you to speak to your daughters tomorrow and hear what they have to say to you."

Mr. Murray stared at Ben but said nothing. His whole body appeared to sag a little.

Ben continued, "I suggest you take this evening to think carefully about what you want to say to your daughters. You may return here tomorrow morning, about eleven, and talk to them then. There is a boardinghouse on the far side of town. If you need assistance with the fee, I will be happy to help you with that."

"No need," said Mr. Murray. "I don't need yer charity! I will see you here at eleven. My girls had better be here!" With that, he walked unsteadily out of the house and headed east, through town.

We conferred amongst ourselves after Mr. Murray left. I said I would speak to my Aunt Rebecca and Lydia and see what they wanted to do. Ben and Jacob said they would speak to Rose and Daniel. Mr. Jamison said he would be happy to return the next day and sit in the background, just in case. He said he thought Mr. Murray seemed unstable. I had great misgivings but did not know what else to do.

The next morning at ten-thirty, Aunt Rebecca and Lydia appeared, both grim-faced. Shortly thereafter, Rose and Daniel arrived along with the sheriff. Jacob and Jesse joined us a few minutes later. We settled in the parlor and served tea while we talked about the strange and sudden reappearance of Joseph Murray.

"We don't know what he wants yet," Aunt Rebecca said. "It is difficult to decide what to do without knowing his intentions."

"That may be true," Lydia said, "but I do not consider that man to be my father. I do not want him in my life."

Rose spoke up. "I want to know why he has shown up now after all these years, with no word and no indication of where he has been. I was only a little girl when the authorities took him away. I have very mixed feelings about this, but I do think he has a right to know he has grandchildren, and the children should know they have a grandpa. However, I want an explanation for what happened and why he disappeared. I know why I grew up without a mother, but no one has ever explained to me why I had to grow up without a father, too." Her eyes welled with tears.

I spoke up: "I am concerned about what he will do if he feels thwarted in his efforts to regain a relationship with his children. I do not think that Mr. Murray is quite right in his mind. But we should, at least, listen to what he has to say."

We heard a knock on the front door and Gladys opened it. Joseph Murray entered the parlor, holding his hat nervously in his hands. He had combed his hair and he had brushed the dust from his travels off his pants and coat. "Good morning ma'am," he said, nodding first at me and then at Aunt Rebecca. "Good morning to you, sir," he said nodding to Ben. Ben stood and held out his hand, which Mr. Murray shook tentatively. He looked around the room, his eyes pausing at Lydia and then Rose.

Lydia stood up and said, in a cold voice, "I am Lydia." "My Lydia!" Mr. Murray said in a choked voice, taking a step toward her. Lydia quickly stepped back.

"I am not 'your' Lydia!" she said in a tight voice. "I am not anyone's Lydia!" She snapped out the words. "Where have you been for the past thirty-five years? Why have you come here now? What do you want?"

"Lydia, dear," my Aunt Rebecca chided softly. "Let the man explain himself."

Rose said, softly, "I am Rose. I was a little child when you left. I have had no father for all these past years. I want to hear what you have to say."

Ben said, "Please, Mr. Murray, sit and take some tea. We all want to hear what you have to say."

Mr. Murray sat in a chair facing the group, still holding his hat in his hands. "I know I have no right to come barging into yer lives, all sudden like," he said. "I am not overly proud of the kind of father I was to you two. I am not proud of my life or of where I have been all these years, but my aim is to make amends if there is any way I can. I am an old man. I fear I may be nearing my last days. Bu I never stopped thinking about my girls, and I swore if I was ever released, I would come looking for the two of you." Tears welled up in his eyes.

"And then I saw that magazine cover and knew at last where to start looking." He stopped and looked at each face before him, settling on Lydia and Rose, in turn. Then he went on, in a low voice. He looked tired and defeated.

"I was angry and bitter for most of the last 35 years but now I can see that my anger and bitterness are no good to me anymore. The fight has gone plumb out of me. I never had no other family than you after my Sallie died," he said. "I don't have no family except you two and nowhere to go."

There was silence among us after that. Then Rose spoke up. "I think my children should know they have a Grand Pappy. I need to discuss this with my husband, Daniel, here, of course, but maybe we can work something out."

"I don't have a father. This man is no one to me!" said Lydia, in a pinched voice.

Mr. Murray spoke, "I can understand your bitterness, Lydia. Perhaps in time, you will begin to know and accept me. Meanwhile, if Rose and her husband agree, I would be grateful to meet their children and learn how to be a Grand Pappy to them."

"We can talk about that another time," Rose said.

All agreed, except Lydia, that Mr. Murray could stay at Green's Boarding House while Rose arranged for him to meet her children. Ben walked to the front door with Mr. Murray and said in a low voice that I could just hear, "A bath and a set of clean clothes will go a long way to improving your chances to make amends with your daughters. I will see that Mrs. Green does right by you."

"Thank you, sir," Mr. Murray said. "That is

mighty kind of you. I will pay you back when I can." I could see that his tears were beginning again.

After Joe Murray left, we all stood around awkwardly, not sure what to do. Lydia looked like she was ready to spit nails while Rose wore an expression that said, "What have I gotten myself into now?"

Mr. Jamison spoke up. "Mr. Murray seems to have an understanding of his position. I personally think he is willing to make amends and we should give him a chance. Naturally, you all must be guided by your own feelings," he said, nodding at Lydia and Rose. "Feel free to call on me anytime if there is a need. Meantime, I will do some investigating and see if I can get any information about where Mr. Murray has been for 35 years."

The following Sunday, after church, Rose invited me to have tea with her at her inn. She had invited Mr. Murray to join her and Daniel to meet the children and wanted me there for moral support. I think all of us were surprised when we saw Mr. Murray walk toward the front door looking much cleaner than before; he had even washed and trimmed his hair and beard. He was also wearing different clothes, somewhat ill- fitting, as he was so thin, but they were, at least, presentable.

Rose and Daniel's four children looked stiff and nervous in their Sunday clothes, standing in a row between their parents. Daniel put out his hand to Mr. Murray and wished him good morning.

"These here are my children, Mr. Murray, mine, and Rose's," Daniel said. "Anna is thirteen, Jason is eleven, David is seven, and Rosalie is five." Each child gave a little curtsey or nod as Daniel mentioned her or his name.

Rose spoke, "Sit down Mr. Murray, uh, Father, and have some tea." Turning to her children, she said, "This is Mr. Joseph Murray, your grandfather. He has been away for a long time, but now he has returned and has asked to meet you. I know this may feel strange at first, but your father and I would like to give each of you a chance to get to know your grandfather and for him to get to know you."

Anne and Jason looked at the floor, but David and Rosalie smiled a little and said that would be all right with them.

Turning back to her father, Rose said, "You will have to understand this will take some time. Your return has been a shock to all of us, but I am hoping that someday you can be a part of this family. Meantime, we have a lot of room at this inn, and you are welcome to come live here in exchange for giving us some help running the place. We can discuss the particulars later. How does that sound?"

Mr. Murray said "I am much obliged, Rose. I will help as best I can. I have a lot to make up to you and Lydia." Daniel and Rose agreed that Mr. Murray could move into one of the back rooms at the inn and help with caring for the livestock and gardening in the summer and other care-taking tasks, as he was able.

Not long after their father's return, Lydia asked to see Rose and me. Her friend Lucy was with her. Lydia told us she had something important to tell Rose in strictest confidence and wanted Lucy and me there as well since we were both present when her father was arrested and sent away so many years ago. We met at my house and I arranged for us not to be disturbed. Lydia was visibly upset but made an effort to be calm.

"Rose," she said, "There is something you must know about our father, something I have never told anyone, not even my most trusted friends, Hannah, and Lucy. It is a secret that has eaten away at me for all of my life." Her voice was shaking, and she paused to compose herself. "You know that our mother died when you were born. I was five and I became your caretaker because our father would not or could not care properly for either of us."

Rose started to say something.

"No, no, I must tell you this! I can't hold it inside any longer now that our Pa has returned." Lydia dashed a tear away from her cheek.

"Pa adored Ma. I remember him being affectionate and kind when I was little. He became distraught and angry after Ma died and started drinking more than before. It was as if something snapped inside of him. He took his rage out on me because I was handy. He used to beat me when he was drunk, which was often. I protected you the best I could. Pa was also very lonely, missing our Ma. I was just a little child—I did not know how to stop him." Lydia began to sob and could not speak for a few minutes. We sat in shocked silence. When she could collect herself, she went on in a whisper,

"He said he would kill me if I ever told anyone." Her face was white. "I will spare you the details," she continued, tears flowing freely. "I truly believe, if we had not been taken from him when we were, I would have killed him! Oh Rose, never leave your children alone with that man, especially Anna and Rosalie. NEVER!"

Rose, Lucy, and I looked at Lydia in horror, and I began to see some of my memories in a new light. Poor, dear Lydia. How could any of us have known? No wonder she feels as she does, now that her father has returned!

Rose threw her arms around Lydia and rocked her, both of them crying now. I knelt on the floor in front of Lydia's chair and held her hands. "I am so sorry, Lydia!" I whispered, "So terribly sorry. We saw the bruises but never guessed there was more, even worse."

Lucy was crying too. "Oh, dearest Lydia—I should have known. I should have done something, told someone. All the times you came to school saying you had tripped over a tree root, how uncomfortable you were with the boys, how frightened you were to wear a new dress home. I had no experience with such things. Oh, my dear! Why didn't you say anything when you got older when your father could no longer hurt you?"

"I was too ashamed," Lydia whispered. "And what good would it have done?"

"What should I do?" Rose asked, stunned. "He is living in our house. We already agreed to take him in since he has nowhere else to go. I have to tell Daniel."

I wondered aloud, "Do you think it is possible for someone to change? It has been more than thirty-five years. He seems so sincere in wanting to make amends. He is an old man now with nowhere to turn ..." I did not know what else to say. No one responded. We held each other and sat for a while in dazed silence. Rose later agreed to limit opportunities for her father to spend time with his grandchildren unless she, Daniel or another adult was present and to never allow any of the children to spend time alone with him. Lydia seemed to feel much better for finally having told her story, and we all agreed that this information need go no further than the four of us.

Chapter Thirty-Three

My fears for Sarah finally came to fruition. I noticed she often did not come right home after school, and sometimes even missed dinner. When I asked Jacob about it, he said he had promised not to tell. I demanded that he tell me, and he finally admitted there were days when Sarah did not go to school at all. In fact, he told me, she had met a young man from Tamworth and was sneaking off to see him.

I was furious but also scared. I told Ben. He was as upset as I was. When Sarah finally returned that night, her cheeks flushed, we sat her down and asked her to explain herself.

"I have met someone—his name is James," she said simply as if that was all that needed to be said.

"And who is James and why have you been seeing him without telling us," Ben said. He was trying to remain calm but failing.

"We knew you might react this way so we decided we should keep it a secret until we were sure," Sarah said defiantly.

"Till you were sure about what," I said, my fears growing.

"We want to leave here and go west to homestead in the Arizona territories," she said. "James has some grand ideas. We are making plans. We will marry on the way," she said with finality.

Suddenly, I saw a vision of my own mother as she might have looked at the same age, having a similar conversation with her parents.

"Oh, dear God," I gasped, involuntarily. "Sarah, Sarah, think carefully about this before you make any rash decisions."

"Our minds are made up. We are leaving next week."

"I thought you said you were not sure," I said, holding back tears.

"We are sure NOW," Sarah said and stood up to go.

"And if we try to stop you?" Ben asked.

"You can't stop us. James is of age—he is twenty-one. And besides, you are not my father!" Sarah threw this remark at Ben and I heard him suck in his breath as if she had physically struck him.

"You are not of age, Sarah," Ben managed to say. "We could have James arrested for seducing a minor or hold you here until you turn eighteen."

"Just try it," she spat. "Besides, my birthday is in a few months. What would be the point?"

"At least, bring James here so we can meet him," I begged. "We know nothing about him! How do his parents feel about this?"

"They don't know yet," Sarah said shortly as she wheeled and left the room.

My mind was in turmoil and Ben paced angrily from one end of the room to the other.

"Oh, Ben. She is almost of age," I said bleakly. "Nothing we say or do will change how she feels. I think we are going to have to let her go." The pain in my heart was almost unbearable. "Oh Ben," I said, clinging to him, "This must be how my grandmother felt when my mother ran off with my father!"

The following week, James presented himself to us at the train station, one hour before the train was due to come through town heading south to Boston. There they would change trains and travel west.

James was a tall, slender man, with dark hair and a small goatee. He was smartly dressed in a traveling suit. For all his bravado, he looked only a couple of years older than our Sarah did. He had little to say to us but did shake Ben's hand and tipped his hat to me. He had two small valises with him, and Sarah had packed only what she could comfortably carry in her one. I pressed a small basket into her hands containing sandwiches and fruit for the journey. Ben had placed an envelope underneath the food, containing a brief note of love from each of us, and $100.00 in small bills.

"We promise we will marry soon," Sarah said. "And we will write." I just nodded and held her tightly in my arms. Then the train came, and they boarded and were gone. In my heart I was thinking, first my uncles, then my mother, and now my own darling Sarah. How can a mother bear such a loss?

A month later, we received a letter postmarked St. Louis, telling us they had married and were expecting a baby. There was no return address and we never heard anything further. My sweet baby was gone.

Journal Entry, June 1898

Dearest Mama - How my heart aches! My Sarah has left us for parts unknown. She is just an impetuous and angry child. I fear we may never see her again. She says she is married but how can we be sure? We do not even know her young man's last name—they clearly do not want anyone to find them. There will be a child born soon—my first grandchild and I may never know him—not even his name. I feel so helpless and lost. Oh, Mama, this is too cruel! I do not know how I can bear it! However, there is nothing I can do so but bear it I must.

Your grieving daughter, Hannah

Chapter Thirty-Four

I know it hurt Ben to see me pine for Sarah. He missed her sorely as well. The children often asked about her, wanting to know when she would be coming back. These were hard questions to answer.

One afternoon, a few weeks after we received Sarah's letter, Ben said he had something to tell me. We were sitting in the parlor enjoying a mid- afternoon respite. The house was quiet with the children still at school.

"I have done something behind your back, Hannah, but I hope you will forgive me when you find out what it is. I decided to ride over to Tamworth yesterday to see if I could find out anything about James and Sarah. I knew it was a long shot, knowing only James' first name and what he looks like, but I figured Tamworth was a small village like ours, and perhaps someone would know of him and his family." I looked at him in surprise.

"Tell me what you found out? Was there anybody who could tell you where they are or how to reach them?"

"I thought the general store would be the best place to start and I was right. Several folks there knew of James and his family, and about what James had done. 'Well,', I told them, 'I am the father of the young woman James ran off with.' I told them Sarah is only seventeen and that we just want to know if she is all right and where the two of them might have gone. I told them, 'Sarah has written to us only once since they left and said they are expecting a baby. We are at our wit's end.'"

"Hannah, they were sympathetic and commiserated with me about our plight. Then one of them, a man named Peterson, told me where I could find James's family. They live on one of the outlying farms west of Tamworth. Their last name is Parker, so at least, we know that. Mr. Peterson offered to go there with me next week and in the meantime, he would see what he could find out on his own. I wanted to talk to you about this first. What do you want me to do?"

"Find out as much as you can without stirring up trouble, and perhaps we can find out more by contacting some of the local papers in the Arizona Territories." I was feeling more hopeful than I had felt since Sarah announced her intentions to leave.

The following week, Ben rode over to Tamworth, taking Jacob with him. The weather was cloudy and very cold, and I urged them to wait a few days. However, in December, the weather can turn at any time and bring heavy snow, so Ben insisted on going. He and Jacob returned late in the evening just as icy sleet had begun to fall. Ben said James' family had received a letter similar to ours but with no further news of their whereabouts. It was discouraging.

"James's family was more receptive to our visit once they knew we were not there to make trouble," Ben told me. "Two of James's brothers, Nat, and Tom, even offered to go west to look for James and Sarah. In fact, I think they were eager for an adventure. Nat said James has been talking for years about going west. He wanted to look for gold and there was not much for him to stick around for on their small farm."

Ben began talking about going out there himself and bringing her home.

"No, no Ben," I said. "We need you here and besides, I doubt they will agree to come back. I do worry so about them and the baby. Perhaps next spring or summer we can consider a trip out to the Territories but not now as winter comes." To my relief, Ben agreed to wait, hoping that more information might come to light in a few months. We determined to be patient.

I decided to prevail upon my business relationship with Mr. Ramsey who published our local newspaper and my patterns. I thought that, with his newspaper connections he might be able to find out something useful for us. I did not know where else to begin.

We heard nothing for many weeks but finally got one tenuous lead. Sarah and James had arrived in Arizona Territory but there was no information regarding where they had settled.

That winter was more difficult than most; heavy snows fell and very few people went out unless they absolutely had to, except for church. Even school was called off when the snow was too deep, and the roads had not been broken out. I felt cooped up as well as anxious over Sarah, and tempers at home were short. I worked on designing and sewing when I could and that helped take my mind off Sarah and her baby.

Chapter Thirty-Five

Everyone breathed a sigh of relief when March 1899 finally arrived, and the snow began to melt in earnest. Of course, we had mud then, everywhere, and getting around was still difficult but everyone's spirits rose as the air grew warmer.

In early April, when the world was turning green, Jacob told me, in confidence, that he had begun courting a young woman in town. He was shy about telling me. He said they were keeping their relationship secret for the time being so that no one could tell them they were too young to be serious.

"But Mama, I felt I should tell you, at least, this much," he said. "I did not want you to be hurt again the way Sarah hurt you and Ben."

"Will you and your new love move away from here?" I asked in a sudden panic.

"No, Mama" he reassured me. "If we do marry, we will live right here in town. Besides," he continued. "I love working with Ben and Uncle Jesse. I want cabinet making to be my life work and I want to continue to live here with you and our family until I marry if that is all right with you."

I was flooded with relief at that and told him I looked forward to meeting this young woman when they were ready to share the news.

A few weeks later, Jacob brought Alice Jenkins and her parents to meet us. Sallie Mae prepared a lovely tea with sandwiches and little cakes and we spent a pleasant afternoon getting to know each other. Soon after that, Alice's parents invited us to dinner at their home so we could meet the whole family.

At eighteen, Alice was petite and pretty. She had a trim figure and long, lustrous brown hair. She was soft-spoken and somewhat shy, but we warmed up to each other quickly. I soon learned she had a lively sense of humor and was intelligent. I could see why Jacob had fallen for her and I felt sure he had chosen wisely. Ben and I were happy to welcome Alice into our family. Because they were both so young, they were in no hurry to marry right away, much to the relief of both families.

One afternoon in early June, Tom and Nat Parker appeared on horseback at our house. They declared that it was time to head west, and asked Jacob if he wanted to go with them to find his sister. I saw that he was torn.

"What do you think I should do?" he asked Ben and me. "There is Alice to consider and a wedding to plan. I have my work with Ben. But I doubt Sarah would ever agree to come home if I do not go."

"It would be best to talk to Alice," Ben said. "If she agrees, then go with my blessing."

"Mine too," I said, giving him a hug.

Two days later, Tom, Nat, and Jacob were on their way. Alice came with Ben and me to the train station to see them off. I gave each young man a warm hug and a hamper filled with food for the journey and some money for travel expenses. Alice and I both wiped away tears.

"I promise to write and let you know what we find out," Jacob said, as he stepped into the train. "Please do not worry. We will be back before you know it!"

What a long summer that was! We received several letters but not much news of Sarah and James. Then finally, in September, there was a telegram: "We found them. Coming home."

Oh, what joy! I could not sit still or concentrate on anything until I knew they were home safe. Alice asked me every day if I knew when they would arrive. She and I began haunting the railway station every afternoon at 2:00 pm when the northbound train was scheduled to arrive.

Then one crisp October day, as the train rolled to a stop at our station, we finally saw a familiar face at the window. It was Jacob! However, when he stepped onto the platform, he was alone.

"Where is Sarah?" I asked before I had even said 'hello". "Where are James and his brothers?" Jacob gave me a quick hug, wrapped his arms around Alice, and kissed her before he spoke. He looked exhausted.

"We found them," Jacob said. "It took some doing, longer than we expected. They said they are happy and do not want to come home, even after I begged them. James is working on a ranch, tending cattle and he loves it. He is making a decent wage. They have a little house of their own not far from the main house with their own vegetable garden and chickens. It is a beautiful place, a wide valley surrounded by mountains. A river cuts through part of the ranch. Tom and Nat liked it so much they decided to stay and hire on as well. There is a comfortable bunkhouse where the unmarried hands live."

I felt a stabbing pain in my heart at Jacob's words. "What about Sarah and the baby?" I asked.

"You have a beautiful little granddaughter," Jacob said. "Her name is Emma. Emma Louise Parker. She is the spitting image of her Ma and her Grandma except she has her father's dark hair. Sarah says she and James are happy and she is content in their new home. She says she is kept busy with the baby and taking care of her garden and chickens." Jacob lowered his voice. "Sarah also said to tell you she is sorry." I burst into tears. Jacob put his arms around me.

"Look here," Jacob said, after a moment. "I have something to show you." He reached into his coat pocket and carefully withdrew a photograph mounted inside a cardboard cover. The name and address of the photographer appeared on the front cover in fancy script. Jacob held it out to me. I was almost afraid to open it. My hands were shaking. In Inside was a formal portrait of my beautiful Sarah and a very handsome

James with little Emma sitting on Sarah's lap. Emma was wearing a sweet little bonnet. I could not stop looking at the photograph. Then I noticed a post office box address for Mr. and Mrs. James Parker, care/of the Patrick McBride, Copper Stallion Ranch on the back cover. I could not breathe for a moment, and I burst into tears once again.

"Thank you, Jacob," I said. "You have no idea how much this means to me."

"I think I do, Mama," he said gently.

A few days later, Ben and Jacob rode over to Tamworth to break the news to the Parkers. I felt badly for them. I lost my daughter, but they lost three sons. At least both our families gained a granddaughter. I wondered if I would ever meet her.

Journal Entry, September 1899

Dearest Mama — I wish you could have seen Ben's face when he heard the news about Sarah and saw the photograph of her little family. My big strong husband broke down and cried. Now, at least, we have an address where we can write to them and Ben says that maybe we can take a trip out to the Territories to visit with them, sometime. I think that would be grand!

I made baby Emma a sweet quilt in bright colors with a label on the back on which I embroidered the following: "Made especially for Emma Louise by your loving Grandmother,

Hannah Benson Stone, fall 1899. Remember always that you are loved." I will send another of my larger quilts out with this one to Sarah and James for their own bed.

I no longer feel that we have completely lost our Sarah and our very first grandchild. What a blessing.

Your much-relieved daughter, Hannah

On a beautiful warm day, the following June, Jacob and Alice were married in the village church exactly twenty-four years after Jacob's father and I were married there. I felt overcome with my own memories, but also with pride for my handsome first-born son and his lovely bride.

Jacob and Alice set up housekeeping in a nearby rented cottage while they prepared to move out to the little farm that Aaron had so lovingly built when he and I were first married. It warmed my heart that they wanted to farm the land once again. They will live in town during the winter months, however. And, as if that were not enough, Alice shared their happy news just a few months later—another grandbaby was on its way!

I was forty-four and beginning to feel old.

Journal Entry, March 1901

Dearest Mama – So much has been happening these past months! My heart is full. Jacob and his Alice married almost a year ago, and have a beautiful baby boy, named Charles Aaron. They call him Charlie. I am happy and grateful that Jacob and his family live nearby and that Jacob continues his work with Ben. That is a great comfort to me. We all love to visit with his growing family on warm summer days when we can go swimming or boating on the pond.

Meanwhile, my other children are growing up so fast! Becky is almost sixteen and Lyddie is twelve. They are both bright and engaging young girls and very pretty. I just wish they had taken to sewing the way I did. Still, I can see a creative spark shining in each of them. Lyddie enjoys drawing and painting. We gave her a set of watercolor paints and colored chalks at Christmas. Becky has taken an interest in photography and we gave her one of the box cameras that are so popular now. It seems every time I turn around, she is taking another photograph.

Benny just turned ten, and Maggie is seven already. Both are doing well in school. Maggie loves to read, and she has begun writing little stories that she enjoys reading aloud to the family. I recently started teaching her to sew and she seems to like it! I am so pleased. I will help her make her first quilt when she is ready.

Benny is helping his father in his woodworking shop in the barn when he is not in school. He appears to have a fascination with building things and Ben is delighted to teach him as much as he can absorb at this age.

Ben is beyond proud of our children, and we are both curious to see how they turn out, as they grow older.

Your grateful daughter, Hannah

·୭ଡ଼ୄ·

Chapter Thirty-Six

The winter of 1903-1904 was particularly difficult. There were several severe snowstorms, one right after the other, and an ice storm in February that brought down many trees. For a time, the storms cut our little village off from the outside world, our only links the telephone at the newspaper office and a handful of other locations. Even the trains had difficulty making their way north or back south and trying to keep the tracks clear and the roads open for sleighs and wagons was a constant battle. Most folks hunkered down in their homes trying to stay warm and did not venture out for days at a time.

The ice storm was particularly destructive. In the sunshine that came a few days later, the trees looked breathtakingly beautiful covered in an inch or more of ice. The branches glittered and glowed when the sun hit them, and everything sparkled as far as you could see. However, a high wind followed the ice storm and many trees simply broke or split apart. Branches of all sizes and even whole trees covered the ground all over town. Here and there, a house or barn roof collapsed under the great weight or was damaged by a fallen tree. It made me sick to think about what might have happened to the forest around our cabin on the lake, and whether the house and barn were all right.

We would have to wait patiently until the snow begins to leave the woods and we could venture in.

Two days after the ice storm, we got the terrible news that a bizarre accident had claimed the life of Mr. Benson. Jesse, his voice shaking, was able to tell us what happened. Mr. Benson had gone out alone to inspect the damage among his prized apple trees on the steep hill where we went sledding as children. When he did not appear for supper, Will and two of their farm hands went out looking for him. It was dark by then and they carried lanterns, the three of them fanning out across the steep and icy slope. They received no response when Will called his father's name. Eventually, they made their way to the bottom of the orchard and there they found Mr. Benson's body. It looked as if he had lost his footing on the glare ice and had hurtled into a pine tree at the very bottom of the hill (one of the ones our parents had warned us about as children). He probably died instantly, and his body had already frozen solid by the time they found him.

I was heartbroken when I heard this news and went up to the Benson farm as soon as I could to see to Martha, Lizzy, and Aaron's brothers and to offer my assistance and deep condolences. I was stricken with this loss more than I ever could have imagined. Mr. Benson was the father I never had but it was not until I lost him that I realized just how important he had been to me. I grieved with the family as if he had been my own father. The family held a memorial service in the village church a few days later with the entire village (it seemed) in attendance, but they decided to wait until spring for a formal internment.

Martha, of course, was inconsolable, and knowing very well how she must feel, I spent as much time with her as I could and urged her to continue being part of the quilting bee so her quilting friends could support her as they had done for me when I was so full of my own grief.

Jesse continued to work with Ben as a cabinetmaker, and I could see daily how much he was hurting. He had idolized his father despite the fact he had chosen a different vocation. Daniel had Rose and his family to help him through his grief, but I felt his pain as well.

I think the loss of his father hit Will the hardest, as the eldest son, and I gave him what support he was able to accept from me. I was proud of the way he took over the running of his father's farm and orchards.

Lizzy was the strongest of all of them. She was steadfast as a loving daughter and sister and continued to help both Will and her mother on the farm. She was like a rock, holding the family together. I sometimes wondered if she resented the fact that she had never married and would likely take care of her family for the rest of her days, as my Aunt Rebecca had, but I never saw any signs that she did.

Journal Entry, February 1904

Dearest Mama — Another wonderful and caring man has left my life and the family he loved so dearly. Aaron's father has left this earth in a most tragic accident. Why is it that the very best are so often taken? I know that is not fair to say — everyone must die eventually. However, I feel his loss in a way I never expected. I am grateful for all the years he was part of my life and for the kinship I have cherished with him, Martha, and his family. I hope you will greet him in heaven and let him know how much we all miss him.

Not all is completely gloomy here. Jacob and Alice had another darling little boy a few months ago to carry on the Benson name for another generation. They named him William Daniel after his grandfather and uncles, but they call him Billy. He is a joy. Little Charlie is devoted to him and tries to carry him around. It is very funny to watch.

It warms and comforts my heart to know that Mr. Benson has three grandsons to keep his name and spirit alive among all of those who loved him so dearly.

Your grieving but grateful daughter, Hannah

Chapter Thirty-Seven

One afternoon in the fall of 1905, I was working in my sewing room at the back of the house, on the second floor. I had enjoyed a productive morning working on a new design and was now at work sewing the blocks I had cut out earlier. The sky had been darkening all afternoon and I had been obliged to light the gas lamps early to help with my sewing. The wind was swaying the trees outside my windows and I could hear the faint boom of thunder in the distance, but I barely noticed, so great was my concentration.

Suddenly I heard an enormous crash and jumped up my heart racing. I looked out the window just in time to see a jagged bolt of lightning slice through the sky somewhere beyond the barn. Then another crash and another jagged flash, even closer. However, there was no sound of rain and the storm moved away almost as quickly as it had come with just a few distant rumbles. I went back to my work.

A bit later, something caught my attention—a strange smell. At first, I paid no heed, but the smell grew stronger. Then I heard a commotion coming from the barn, the sounds of animals in distress. I looked out the window towards the barn and saw, to my horror, a wisp of smoke coming from the barn roof.

"Dear God!" I exclaimed. "Fire!" For a moment, I stood transfixed, not believing what I was seeing; then I ran through the house calling for Gladys and Sallie Mae. Thank goodness, the children were in school.

"Sallie Mae," I screamed when I saw her coming toward me, "Run quick to those new cottages by the lake and fetch Mr. Stone and Jesse. They need to come right away! The barn is on fire! Spread the word!" Then I raced outside to the barn and opened the heavy doors.

By this time, the horses and goats were frantic. I heard their screams and the sound of their hoofs beating against the walls of their stalls. The smoke was thick inside the barn, but I crawled across the floor until I reached the stall doors and unlatched them. I saw flames above my head and embers were flying, igniting new blazes in other parts of the hayloft.

As the horses and goats rushed past me, I heard voices and the sound of people running toward me. The fire spread quickly now. I ran outside to open the chicken coop behind the shed. I saw our neighbors forming a bucket brigade, passing water from hand to hand across the road from the lake to our house. There was no fire department in those days, no hoses, ladders, or any other equipment.

Ben ran toward me. "Are you all right, Hannah?"

"Yes, Ben, yes!" I yelled, "But we are going to lose

the barn! We have to save the house!" Jesse and Jacob came right behind Ben.

"Get the horses," I yelled at them, "See if you can round up the goats and the chickens." I was frantic, then, calling for our cats. There was thick smoke everywhere and visibility was terrible.

By this time, almost everyone from the village had converged to help battle the flames and to pull valuables from the house.

"Watch out for the shed roof," I heard someone yell. It was clear we could not save the barn and the shed was in flames as well. The heat was unbearable. Embers flew everywhere.

"Ben," I screamed, "We have to save what we can! Help me carry our things from the house!"

Sallie Mae, Gladys, and I ran upstairs and grabbed handfuls of clothing, quilts, and whatever small valuables we could. There were quilt racks in two of the bedrooms and we grabbed as many of those quilts as could manage. Several men helped Ben carry out furniture. Flames were already licking up the back of the house.

"Ben, my sewing machine!" We had little time to spare.

Ben and Jacob passed me on the way to my sewing room. The machine, with its cast iron legs and treadle, was very heavy but they managed to get it out of my sewing room and downstairs just as the flames reached through the back walls of the house and the curtains in my sewing room caught fire.

There were people everywhere, carrying china, rugs, and dining room chairs, piling everything in front of the house near the road. Someone had picked up Ben's dollhouse and saved it. I burst into tears when I saw it on the ground.

"Look out!" someone yelled. "The roof has caught!" In what was likely only seconds but felt like slow motion, the fire engulfed the entire house. Acrid smoke blew everywhere, and I ran blindly towards the road and away from my beautiful home.

"Ben, Ben"! I screamed, "Jacob! Where are you? Where are my babies?" I stumbled and someone caught me. It was Jacob.

"Where is Ben?" I asked in a hoarse voice. I wanted to run back to the house, but Jacob held me tightly.

"No, Mama, no!" There was a roaring noise and then the sound of windows exploding. I thought I must be in a terrible nightmare and tried to wake but found that I could not. It was all too real.

The bucket brigade ceased. All anyone could do then was to stand helplessly and watch as the roof of our beautiful home collapsed, and the walls caved in. Ben found me and wrapped his arms around me as we watched the destruction of our dreams. Gladys had fetched the children from school and brought them over to us. We stood with our arms around each other. We were in shock. No one made a sound, not even a whimper.

Soon, all that was left of the world we had known was a haphazard pile of personal belongings. I spotted my sewing machine in the pile and saw that one end of the wood case was charred. I looked at Ben's hands, then, and saw burns on them as well. They were already starting to blister.

"Oh Ben—I am so sorry," I said softly. "Your hands."

"It is nothing," he said, pulling his hands away. "The most important thing is that you and the children and everyone who helped us are safe and unharmed."

One by one, our friends and neighbors stopped by our numb family group and offered their condolences. Every one of them gave us assurances that they would help in any way they could in the coming days and weeks. Gradually, the crowd thinned out as everyone went sadly home.

Then Aunt Rebecca was there with Lydia and Lucy. Daniel was nearby with Rose. They had brought the carriage and wagons. Aunt Rebecca gently urged us to come away to their house to rest. Ben and Jacob piled our furnishings in the wagon and carried them sadly to her house. Jane and her mother arrived soon after with a fully prepared hot supper to nourish and comfort us.

"Tomorrow is soon enough to decide what to do," Rebecca said, as she hugged each one of us in turn and urged us to try to get some sleep.

CARY FLANAGAN

Chapter Thirty-Eight

Ben was up at dawn the next morning, a look of resolute determination on his face. I could barely summon the energy to sit up in bed after I remembered what had happened the day before.

"What are you doing, Ben," I asked as he dressed. "Where are you going?"

"To our house," he said. "It is time to clean up and begin anew." My Ben—he never ceased to astonish me. I wondered where he got his strength. For that entire day and the difficult days that followed, the look of resolve and determination never left his face.

I joined Ben a while later at the still smoking ruins of our house. Several of our friends and neighbors had already arrived and were pitching in to help clear the rubble where it was cool enough to handle.

Jesse had gone up to the Benson farm the night before to tell them what had happened and to get our livestock to safety. He reappeared with Will the next morning. Daniel and Rose were already there doing what they could. Mrs. Benson and Lizzy arrived soon after in a wagon laden with food, cider, and fresh water for the work crews.

There was nothing left to salvage from any of the structures except the bricks from the two chimneys and the granite foundation stones. Even the sturdy cast iron kitchen stove and the other woodstoves that had heated the house through ten long winters were now just piles of shapeless iron. Gradually, using rakes and shovels, our friends cleared the area where the house, shed and barn had once stood and hauled the debris away.

Toward late afternoon, I heard a plaintive mewing sound coming from somewhere nearby, and I found our sweet momma cat and one of her babies cowering under a bush in our neighbor's yard. Black soot covered them, but they did not appear to be injured. I picked them up and carried them over to Mrs. Benson and Lizzy to look after until we could get them to Aunt Rebecca's house. There was no sign of the other two kittens.

In my darkest moments, thinking about all we had lost, I forced myself to concentrate on how much we still had, how blessed we were that no one was killed or injured. Most of all, how lucky we were to have such generous friends and neighbors—even strangers—who pitched in to help us in our hour of greatest need. That was no small thing!

Over the next days and weeks, many of the folk with whom we had done business in the past offered building materials and supplies at their cost, sometimes even free of charge. Clothing for adults and children, furniture, bedding, pots, and pans— friends and strangers alike offered all these to us with a smile. It was humbling to realize how many people reached out to us, in so many ways, to help our family recover from this tragedy.

Thank the good Lord that my four youngest children were strong and resilient. They had weathered the horror of losing their home and all their personal possessions with equanimity much like that of their father. Even ten-year-old Maggie, who lost her favorite doll, seemed to understand that possessions might not be permanent.

I was beyond proud of each of my children as they faced and learned to accept what had happened. The hardest thing was losing the kittens. There were tears shed for them. But the horses, goats, and chickens were being well cared for at the Benson's farm until we could move them back to our new home, once it was finished. We were all moving forward, no easy task.

It was quite a challenge to fit our family of eight into Aunt Rebecca and Lydia's house. We doubled up on all the bedrooms and had three treadle sewing machines set up. I moved mine into the parlor so as not to disturb the thriving dressmaking business. My aunt did less and less of the active work in their business, now. At eighty-two, she was clearly slowing down, although she was still sharp in her mind. I do think that having so many people around her, especially the children, was a stress for her. She never complained to us directly. However, every week or two she would ask how the work on our new house was progressing.

"I can't wait to see your beautiful new house," she would say.

I continued to design and make new quilts as best I could under the circumstances. Thank goodness, my sewing machine was still in perfect working order after I cleaned off all the soot. There was only a minor charring on the end of the wood case. Ben continued to work on a few outside projects but focused mostly on planning and building our new house. The children continued their schooling. Life went on.

We needed income to cover all our expenses and I made up my mind that as soon as the new house was finished and our lives returned to "normal," I would create and publish a catalog of all my quilt patterns (fifteen now). I was grateful that Mr. Ramsey had saved the originals of each pattern he had published for me, so even though the fire destroyed my stock I could go on. He graciously offered to reprint a dozen copies of each of my patterns at no charge and we discussed how to design and print a catalog when I was ready. What a generous soul.

One morning, Aunt Rebecca did not appear for breakfast. Lydia went up to check on her and found her still in bed, looking confused and unable to speak clearly. She was in considerable distress. We summoned the doctor right away but there was little he could do for her. He told us she had had a major stroke, which left her paralyzed all down one side. I held her cold hands and spoke to her, telling her how much I loved her and how much I appreciated her for raising me. Lydia and Rose were there as well; they each shared their love and gratitude for all the years Aunt Rebecca had cared for and supported them. I do not know how much of this she heard or understood, but it was comforting to hold her hands and talk to her. I hoped she could feel our love.

We held a vigil beside her bed, giving everyone who wanted to a chance to visit briefly and to say goodbye. My aunt floated in and out of consciousness, then finally let go and went to meet her Maker. Although I knew this day would come, I was not ready to let her go. I could not stop crying.

The whole town turned out for Rebecca's funeral and we had the largest procession I had ever seen walking to her gravesite in the old cemetery beside the church. Rebecca was well known and much loved and admired by many people. Even those who had not met her personally turned out to pay their respects. She would have been embarrassed to see such a fuss made over her.

I inherited the house. Lydia inherited my aunt's two sewing machines and her dressmaking business. I invited Lydia to stay on in the house as long as she wanted, as our family would soon have our new house finished. With my blessing, she invited her dear friend, Lucy Hastings, to come and live with her and keep her company after our family moved out. Lucy decided to retire from teaching so she could help Lydia with her dressmaking. I was delighted that the two of them still shared such a strong bond after all these years and that my aunt's dressmaking business would continue in such capable hands.

Both Lydia and Lucy wanted to continue hosting

our monthly bee meetings, for which the members were grateful. The first few meetings I went to after Aunt Rebecca's passing felt strange without her there. She left an enormous empty space in our group. There was not a dry eye among us as we each recalled some of our favorite stories involving Aunt Rebecca.

Journal Entry, October 1905

Dearest Mama – I feel such a pain in my heart after losing my beloved Aunt Rebecca. She was my strength and my light every day of my life after you left us. We have lived in her house since the fire and I guess with everything that has happened in these past months, life became too much for her. She suffered a massive stroke and slipped away a few days later. I feel devastated by this loss but also comforted by the belief that she will join you in heaven at last. Take good care of her for me.

Your grieving daughter, Hannah

Chapter Thirty-Nine

By the spring of 1906, the new house was ready for us with the shed and barn completed soon after that. It was almost an exact replica of our previous house with several important changes. Sheet metal covered every roof and firewalls protected the house, shed, and barn. Ben had added other modern features for our comfort, as well.

Lydia, Lucy, and Rose joined us for our first grand tour. I so wished my aunt had been with us — she would have loved this house! There was a modern kitchen with a shiny new cast iron wood stove and a large pantry, a comfortable parlor and dining room, each with its own ornate wood stove for heat. Tall windows let light pour in from the east, south, and west, giving each room a bright and airy feel. Ben had lovingly set up his remarkable replica dollhouse in a place of honor in the parlor.

There were now five bedrooms instead of seven since Jacob and Sarah no longer lived with us. The children raced excitedly from one bedroom to the next, making claims on which room they wanted for their own. No more sharing bedrooms as we had done at

Aunt Rebecca's house! A large, covered veranda graced two sides of the house facing the lake. A lovely circular extension jutted out from one corner, topped with a turreted roof. Fancy carved "gingerbread" decorated the underside of the veranda roof as well as under the eaves. A huge skylight at the center of the roof flooded the third-floor playroom with light.

As we toured all three floors and saw the new furnishings that replaced what we had lost mixed in with what we had been able to save, it felt to me somehow otherworldly. It was my house but not quite my house. I felt unsettled at first but soon got used to it and loved everything I saw.

Best of all, and saved for last, was my new sewing room. I was overjoyed to see it was much larger than my old one and had more windows. It was on the first floor, overlooking where I planned to plant my new flower gardens. There was plenty of counter space for designing and laying out patterns and quilts and ample storage for my fabrics and notions. A large roll-top writing desk and cabinets stood against one wall to hold completed patterns and paperwork for my business. My beautiful sewing machine stood in a place of honor in the corner. It had bright natural light from large windows on two sides. Two handsome electrified floor lamps added additional light. It was perfect in every way!

Although I had toured the house several times while it was under construction, this room was a great surprise. Ben beamed as he watched me explore. I felt giddy with pleasure and did a little dance around the room.

"Ben, you are a treasure," I exclaimed. "You think of everything! Thank you, thank you." I threw my arms around his neck, then whispered "I love you so much. What can I ever do to repay you?"

"Just be you," he said softly. "Just continue to be the extraordinary woman that you are!" He kissed me, right there in front of the children. I heard them whoop with laughter to see such behavior from their parents.

Journal Entry, June 1906

Dear Mama — We moved into the new house just in time to celebrate Ben's fiftieth birthday. Two major milestones! We invited family, friends, and everyone who had helped and supported us during this past year to a grand Open House and festival in honor of Ben and our beautiful new home.

Jacob supervised a pig roast, and our many guests brought enough food to feed an army. Best of all our children and grandchildren and all the Bensons were there to help us celebrate. I only wish Sarah and her family could have been with us, but she has been writing every month or two and I feel we are becoming closer now. I am hoping Ben and I can travel out this fall to visit her and her growing family. I feel truly blessed many times over. I am happier now than I have been in many months!

Your happy and contented daughter, Hannah.

There were two final journal entries:

Journal Entry, January 1940

Dearest Mama – This time, I do not know if I can go on, even though I know I must. Yesterday at dusk, I went looking for Ben when he did not come in to get ready for dinner. I found him lying curled up in the snow beside the chopping block where he had been splitting and stacking cordwood most of the day. My darling Ben, second love of my life, died just as he had lived, caring for the needs and comfort of his family. Rest in peace, my dearest love. I will join you soon.

Hannah

Journal Entry, May 1949

Dearest Mama – The final curtain is coming down on my life in this little village (though not as little as it was when I was young). My 90th birthday celebrations are over and all my children, grandchildren, and many friends have come to say goodbye to this house. They promise to visit me often in my new home for which I am grateful. They have already taken away what furniture, quilts, and household goods they wish to keep. Everything else of any value, other than a few things I wish to keep for myself, have been sold and have either been taken away or are waiting here for the new owners of the house. The moving men will be here soon to pack up my treasured sewing machine and personal belongings for the move to Conway.

I have spent most of this day going from room to empty room, my cane tapping loudly on the bare floors. I can still hear the echoes of the children's laughter and feel the warmth of happier times. I can sense my darling Ben near me, just out of sight, and each of my children. Their love surrounds me. Even Sarah – I can still see her as a young woman, yearning to find her place in the world, which she did at last.

So many memories fill this space. I feel overwhelmed at the thought of leaving, but I know it is time. No one in the family wants such a large home. It is too difficult to heat and keep up.

A lovely young couple from Boston has purchased the

property and they plan to open a small inn. They want to fix it up and return it to its former elegance. I am glad. They even purchased some of the furniture that has been here for so many years, including antiques from our first house that burned. I was astonished (and grateful) when they offered me a very handsome sum for the replica dollhouse so lovingly made by Ben. I am happy it will continue to bring joy to others and be well cared for. Perhaps someday I will return to visit the inn, but I doubt it.

My new home is with my granddaughter Rachel and her family. I look forward to spending time with my grandchildren (with a new one on the way) and I think I will indulge in a nice long rest. I have earned it!

Your loving daughter, Hannah

Epilogue

Becca put down the manuscript and shook her head in awe at the story she had just read. The final two journal entries had brought her to tears and she sat for a while, hugging the manuscript to her chest, letting her mixed feelings of admiration and grief roll over her.

Over the next few days, with the help of her boyfriend Matt, Becca settled the treadle sewing machine in a place of honor in her living room, near the large windows at the far end of the room. The light was excellent and would be just right for sewing by daylight.

"I think Granny Hannah would have approved of this placement," she mused. "I will be able to sew, just as she did, without the use of modern conveniences."

She found spools of ancient thread and many needles, bobbins, and presser feet in one of the cabinet drawers. She even found the original manual, much to her surprise, but the pages were saturated with oil and so fragile she was afraid to open it. She set about teaching herself how to use this precious machine.

Thoughts about how she might be able to honor Granny Hannah and share her stories and her gifts with others continued to circulate around her brain. Sometimes they rested quietly on the edge of her consciousness as she went about her daily tasks, other times an idea would pop up and she would try to grab onto it before it vanished again. She began filling the pages of a small notebook as each new idea arrived.

Becca looked at Hannah's designs and patterns many times. After much thought, she decided she would share the patterns with her quilting bee friends at their next meeting. She had been teaching her eight-year-old niece, Emma, to sew for the past few months and she decided Emma should be part of this project as well. After all, she would be the sixth generation in her family to become a quilter!

She would ask her bee friends to make quilt blocks and quilts from these patterns and then she could publish the patterns in a book. She would include some of the stories told by members of Hannah's quilting bee. Her friends could piece some of Hannah's quilt designs from reproduction fabrics but perhaps they could also use contemporary fabrics to appeal to a contemporary audience. That would take more thought.

Becca knew she could easily draft out diagrams and instructions for the quilt that she had inherited. Then she remembered the detailed description of Hannah's wedding quilt in the manuscript.

"I am sure I can come up with a design that is close," she thought. Becca began to feel excited about the possibilities.

"Maybe we could have a special exhibition of these antique inspired quilts somewhere, maybe even take them on tour!" she thought. "Maybe I should check out the inn that my great great grandfather built for his family and where Granny Hannah designed and made her quilts while raising her family. It might be a great place to display the quilts and tell her story. It might even be a great place to hold quilt retreats!"

She laughed aloud and did a little dance around the room.

"If you are going to dream, you may as well dream BIG! Right? Now I will start talking to people and make some plans. This is going to be fun!"

Timeline Hannah's Legacy, Book I

This Timeline follows the important dates and events in Hannah Stone's life and continues with her descendants up to the present time. Important or interesting historic events that would have had a bearing on her life and the times in which she lived are also included. *(In italics)*.

1820-1860

1823   **Hannah Caroline Jackson (1805-1859) marries Charles Ira Horner (1802-1860)**

They have three children:

Rebecca Anne Horner

("Aunt Rebecca") (1824 – 1906)

Charles Ira Horner Jr. (1827 -?)

Victor James Horner (1827 -?)

*Caroline Rachel (1834-1863)

1844   **Charles and Victor go west to escape their father and make a new life for themselves.**

1839 – 1860   *The Daguerreotype was invented by Louis Daguerre and introduced in 1839. It was popular from the 1840s to late 1850's, when it was supplanted by newer and less expensive processes.*

1846   *Elias Howe granted a patent on his new sewing machine in Hartford, CT. It was the first sewing machine in the United States and was used in factory assembly lines.*

1850   *Harriet Beecher Stowe's "Uncle Tom's Cabin" is serialized in the National Era, an abolitionist magazine. It was available in book form two years later.*

1850   **Caroline Rachel Horner marries Jacob Matthew Applegate (1830-1861)**

They have one living child after several miscarriages and a still birth:

*Hannah Rebecca Applegate (1858-1951)

1850s   *Sewing machine production became widespread, with the first salable machines being made by Isaac Singer and used commercially.*

1856   *A quotation in Godey's Ladies' Book states: "Next to the plough, this sewing machine is perhaps humanity's most blessed instrument."*

1860 - _____

1860   *First published in 1830, Godey's Ladies Book becomes the most popular journal of its time, with 150,000 subscribers by 1860. The*

*magazine is best known for the hand-tint-
ed fashion plate that appeared at the start of
each issue and which provide a record of the
progression of women's dress over the years.
Along with articles and stories of interest
to women, almost every issue also included
an illustration and pattern with measure-
ments for a garment to be sewn at home.*

1860s   *Sewing machines were first purchased by
the public, especially by women. Work that
took 14 ½ hours (such as making a man's
shirt) was reduced to one hour by machine.
Isaak Singer was the first entrepreneur of
sewing machines that could be purchased on
a monthly payment plan.*

1861   *The Civil War Begins*

1861   **Matthew Applegate enlists in the
Union Army and is killed 6 months
later in Tennessee. His body is never
found.**

1862   **Caroline Applegate catches fever and
dies.**

1862   **Hannah is taken to live with "Aunt
Rebecca" Horner.**

1862   *Abraham Lincoln issues the Emancipation
Proclamation.*

1863   *The Singer Manufacturing Company sells
20,000 sewing machines per year.*

1865   *The Civil War ends. President Abraham
Lincoln is assassinated.*

1870   **Joseph Murray, father of Lydia and Rose, is arrested and sent away. Lydia and Rose go to live with "Aunt Rebecca" Horner.**

1877   **Hannah Applegate marries Aaron Matthew Benson (1857-1883)**

           They have two children:

           Jacob William Benson (1878-1960)

           Sarah Rachel Benson (1881-1954)

1882   **Aaron Benson is killed in a lumbering accident.**

1887   **Hannah Applegate Benson marries Benjamin Whitmore Stone (1855-1939)**

           They have four children:

           Rebecca Caroline Stone (1888-1918)

           Lydia Jane Stone (1890-1972)

           Benjamin Thomas Stone (1892-1965)

           *Margaret Abigail Stone (1895-1970)

1888   *Kodak introduces the first easy to use box camera, with the slogan "You push the button, we do the rest!"*

1889   *First electrified sewing machine invented.*

1895	**Ben Stone finishes building a new house for his family.**
1898	**Sarah goes west to the Arizona Territories with her fiancé James Parker.**
1898	**Sarah Benson marries James Parker in Flagstaff**

They have one child:

Emma Louise

1900- 1940

1900	*Kodak introduces the first Brownie camera. It is an inexpensive "point and shoot."*
Early 1900s	*Electric sewing machines became popular and easily available.*
1905	**Hannah and Ben's house and barns burn to the ground.**
1906	**"Aunt Rebecca" Horner dies.**
	Hannah inherits the house. Lydia
	inherits the dress making business.
1906	**Ben completes building a new house for his family.**
1937	**Ben Stone dies.**

1941   ***Rachel Horner Bradley marries**
George Lawrence Patterson (1915 -)
They have three children:
George Lawrence Patterson (1943 -)

Rebecca Bradley Patterson (1945 -)

*Hannah Applegate Patterson (1949 -)

1941   *The United States enters World War Two*
1945   *World War Two ends.*

1948   **Hannah Stone moves to Concord NH**
to live with her granddaughter,
Rachel and her family.

1951   **Hannah Benson Stone dies.**

1973   ***Hannah Applegate Patterson marries**
William John Taylor
They have three children:
Margaret Rachel Taylor (1975 -)

*Rebecca Anne Taylor (1979 – "Becca")

William Benjamin Taylor (1982 - "Will")

2005   Becca Taylor receives the antique
treadle sewing machine from her
grandmother, Rachel Bradley that had
belonged to her gr. gr. grandmother,
Hannah Benson Stone.
Becca also receives Hannah's quilt,
patterns, and her life story, as dictated
to her granddaughter, Rachel Bradley
in 1951.

* = Direct line of descent

Author's Notes:

The idea for this story came to me from a typewritten manuscript I found among the letters, diaries and family mementos that have been stored away for many generations of my own family. In the faded and fragile pages of this manuscript are the words of a distant great aunt who was born in the early 1800s and who dictated the story of her life to a granddaughter in 1916 when she was about 92. Her parents died when she was young and a wealthy family of cousins took her in and raised her in Medford, Massachusetts.

I borrowed this concept but based Hannah's story on many of my own life experiences and those of people I have known. The overall theme of Hannah's story is loss and resilience, and the courage it takes to learn, grow, and move forward despite life's storms.

Like Hannah, my father was killed when I was an infant, leaving my mother a widow with three little children. Although we did not physically lose our mother when he died, she became emotionally unavailable for each of us for a long time. She remarried when I was almost four.

The details and circumstances of these events in my life are different in Hannah's story, but I do draw heavily on my experiences of growing up in a family grappling with overwhelming grief and anger as well as the complexities of living in a "blended family" with a stepfather.

Long after I had written most of this story, I learned that my maternal grandmother, Sarah, had a Singer treadle sewing machine on which own my mother and sister learned to sew. My sister still has the beautiful carved wood drawers from my grandmother's treadle case, but she has no memory of how or when she acquired them or what became of the actual treadle machine.

The small town in New Hampshire where this story is set is a real place, but it can stand in for any small New England town of its time. My family has summered in a log cabin on a small lake in this township since long before I was born, and I am familiar with the area and its surroundings.

My mother designed the cabin and my parents built it from the trees on the property with the help of local builders. I can visualize the building of Aaron and Hannah's cabin because I have photographs of our cabin under construction in the late 1930s.

A local road crew constructed the road to our cabin just as described in this story except that our road crew was able to use heavy equipment rather than oxen to remove tree stumps and large rocks and to dig and carry gravel from the gravel pit to spread on the road. (That pit is now full of mature trees!) The road is still just a narrow and very bumpy road almost a mile long. Leland Drew, the father of Linda Drew Smith, the current VP of the Madison Historical Society, was part of the crew that built this road. He was seventeen at the time.

I used a few actual place names and features but took liberties to change details and to fictionalize the town to suit my story. I also incorporated historical facts such as when the railroad first brought trains through the center of town. I researched the early history of this village and neighboring townships to help lend authenticity to my story.

The one-room schoolhouse that the children attended in the story still exists and belongs to the town's historical society. It is currently used for civic and community group meetings. Another, smaller schoolhouse once stood beside the dirt road that borders the southeast corner of my family's property. The town erected this tiny school in 1859 and then simply abandoned it after the last class that was held there, about 1900.

We recently located the remains of the long-buried structure, and we recovered many rusted hand-forged nails and part of an iron hinge from the site. This schoolhouse appears on a town map of Madison from 1892, and the school attendance records for that school still exist in the historical society archives.

On a hill nearby, an old road leads to an abandoned farm. All that remains are the stone foundations of the house and barn, now filled with large trees. The stone-lined well is nearby. There are numerous stone walls laid out through the surrounding woods, indicating where there used to be open pastures for sheep and cattle. A stand of old apple trees still survives below the house. We believe whoever lived at the farm abandoned it in the 1880's but we have no information about when it was built, who lived there, or why they left. That may be another story! Life on a farm in New Hampshire was hard in those days.

The story of the Benson apple farm is true, (except for minor details), including the part about Indians who camped out in the kitchen in front of the fireplace on a very cold night. The actual farm is in Maine and has been occupied by the same family since the late 18th century.

My husband and I lived in a 19th century farmhouse in Bristol NH during the 1970's. The house and post and beam barn were built around 1840. There

was a shed connecting the house to the barn and yes –
there was a two-seat privy at the back of the shed!

We were full-time production potters with our
studio in the house and retail shop in the barn during
our years there. We had enormous gardens back then
and put up many jars of preserved and frozen vegetables to tide us through the winter months. We even
raised pigs for a few years (but no goats or chickens)!
We heated primarily with wood. We helped a local
farmer tap his sugar maple trees and boil down the
syrup every March. We had a small apple orchard
and made many gallons of fresh apple cider in the fall
with some friends, using their antique wood apple
press. It was a satisfying life but extremely hard work.
I am grateful we were not trying to live that life in the
1870's!

Bradford Academy in Massachusetts was an
actual school for teachers in the mid-to-late 1800s
and later became Bradford Junior College. My grandmother Sarah graduated from there with a teaching
degree in 1895 or 1896 and taught in a school for
several years in the South before her marriage in Ha-
nover, New Hampshire, in 1904. She was the one who
told me that the students had to sleep three to a bed!

Like Hannah, Rachel, and Becca, I am a quilter and quilt pattern designer who started sewing at
a young age. My mother taught me on her 1950s era
Singer sewing machine, which I still have and treasure.

Hannah is someone I admire both for her
courage and for her resilience in the face of a difficult
life, her devotion to family, and for her creative spirit.
I want to share her story in hopes that she will inspire
others, as well.

About the Author:

Cary Flanagan has been a quilter since 1991. After a twenty-year career in Mental Health and Social Services she left full-time work in 2004 to become a quilt pattern designer, author, and teacher. She established Something Sew Fine Quilt Design at that time. Her work sells nationally and Internationally.

Cary was born and raised in Cambridge Massachusetts. She and her husband, Ron, moved to New Hampshire in 1971 where they spent eleven years renovating a 19th century farmhouse and barn. They moved to their current location in southern New Hampshire in 1982.

Cary has spent almost every summer of her life at the "little log cabin by the lake" and the small village in New Hampshire where her family has spent their summers and where this story is set. These are places she knows well and loves.

Cary holds a BA in Sociology and Anthropology and an M.Ed. in Counseling.

For more information, go to
www.caryflanagan.com
or to
www.somethingsewfine.com.

You can also visit Cary
on Facebook and Instagram.

References and Interesting Reading:

Annual Old Home Day Souvenir Programs for 1902, 1903, 1904, and 1910 Madison NH Historical Society

100th Annual Madison Old Home Week, August 3-11, 2002 (Program) 150th Anniversary of the establishment of Madison, New Hampshire as a separate township from Eaton, New Hampshire (Chartered in 1764) The population of Madison in 1860 was 826 and dropped to 482 in 1920. As of the time of this writing, the population was about 2,504.

A Brief History of Madison, New Hampshire Compiled by the Public Schools of Madison, assisted by Madison Men's Club 1925-26

A History of Conway, New Hampshire Barbara Smart Lucy, Thesis submitted for M.Ed. Degree, Plymouth State College, 1963

Among the Giant Pines – The Century Old Summer Houses of Silver Lake, Roy Bubb. Copyright 2013 Madison Historical Society, Madison New Hampshire

Archives of the Historical Societies, town libraries, and websites for Conway, Madison, and Tamworth, New Hampshire, via the Internet

Around Madison Corner – Around 1860 Leon Gerry, Minuteman Press, North Conway, NH 1979. Reprinted 2007

Hearts and Hands – The Influence of Women & Quilts on American Society Pat Ferrero, Elaine Hedges, and Julie Silber The Quilt Digest Press, San Francisco, copyright, 1987

Helping Children Cope with Separation and Loss Claudia L. Jewett The Harvard Common Press, Harvard, Massachusetts, Inc., 1982

Internet Searches: antique treadle machines, Civil War, New Hampshire history, Victorian and vintage accessories, clothing, houses, quilts and quilt blocks, and other related materials.

More than Petticoats–Remarkable Massachusetts Women Laura Rogers Seavey the Globe Pequot Press, copyright 2005

Places of Historic and Scenic Interest in Carroll County, New Hampshire Compiled by Historical Societies of Carroll County, 2006

Quilts–Their Story and How to Make Them ("America's First Quilt Book") Marie D. Webster (Originally published in 1915) A New Edition with notes and biography of the author by Rosalind Webster Perry, Practical Patchwork, Santa Barbara, CA 1990

Quilts in the Attic – Uncovering the Hidden Stories of the Quilts We Love, Karen S. Musgrave Voyager Press, Minneapolis, MN, copyright 2012.

The White Hills –Their legends, Landscape, and Poetry Thomas Starr King, Published Estes and Lauriat, Boston, 1887

The White Mountains: A Handbook for Travelers M. F. Sweetser, Editor (First published in 1876) Houghton, Mifflin and Company, Boston and New York 1891 (11th edition, revised and enlarged.)

The White Mountains the Old Photographs Series Compiled by Randall H. Bennett, Copyright 1994 Published by Alan Sutton, Inc. Augusta ME

The Quilt Gary Paulson, a Yearling Book, Random House, 2002

This I Accomplish: Harriet Powers Bible Quilt and Other Pieces Kyra E. Hicks, copyright 2008 Black Threads Press

Uncle Tom's Cabin or life among the lowly Harriet Beecher Stowe (1811-1896) First published in book form in 1852, John P. Jewett & Co., Boston and Jewett, Proctor & Worthington, Cleveland, Ohio

Visions from a White Mountain Palette – the Life and Times of Charles A. Hunt, Madison's White Mountain Painter Roy Bubb. Peter E. Randall Publisher LLC, Portsmouth NH, 2009291

When I was a Little Girl Elizabeth Cummings Qualey–written for her children and grandchildren. Copyright 1981, Carlton C. Qualey Reprinted by the

Madison Historical Society, Minutemen Press

Sarah's Quest:
A Place to Belong
Book II of Hannah's Legacy

By Cary Flanagan

PART I

Chapter One: June 1898

My stomach churned. I dug my fingernails into the palm of my hands to try to make it stop. "Please," I said softly, "please don't let me throw up!" I couldn't sleep a wink the night before and had too many butterflies in my stomach to eat any breakfast this morning knowing what I was about to do.

It was one of those mornings that could not make up its mind: blue sky with scudding clouds one minute, making way for sullen gray skies the next. Just when you thought rain would start, the sun would break through again. There was a light breeze, and it felt cool for June. It was the kind of day Mama liked to call 'fidgety.' *Oh, Mama.* My heart lurched along with my stomach.

And there we were, standing stiffly together while we waited for the train to pull in, Mama, Ben, my little sister Becky who had insisted on coming, James looking handsome and dapper in his brown tweed traveling suit and bowler hat, and me. I had purchased my gray traveling suit just for this trip, but I felt strange wearing it, as if it had been made for somebody else.

My plain straw hat perched awkwardly on the pile of my blond hair. I did not know what to do with my hands.

Ben reached out to James to shake his hand. James shook it but evaded Ben's eyes.

"Where are your parents or other members of your family?" Ben asked. "Didn't they want to meet your fiancée and see you off?"

"They did not want to make the trip over from Tamworth," James said. "We said our goodbyes at the house. And besides, I think they are happy to see me gone."

Ben looked surprised but did not pursue the question as we heard the train approaching in the distance. "Take good care of my daughter," Ben said, with a pained expression. James nodded but said nothing. Mama had a handkerchief to her eyes. Becky had grabbed my hand and did not want to let go.

"Please, Sarah," she said. "Please don't go." I gave her hand a squeeze and smiled at her. There really was no more to say. I looked briefly at James and he gave me a tight smile. Sunlight crept between the clouds at that moment, but the air around us chilled me.

Finally, we heard the whistle of the train and the chugging sounds as it rolled slowly to a stop. While passengers stepped off the train around us, we hastily said our goodbyes. Mama gave me a tight hug and whispered, "I pray the lord keeps you safe and brings you back to us someday. I love you." Tears ran down her cheeks, and I gave her a quick kiss as I turned away.

I could not look directly at Ben, but I mumbled, "Take care of her and keep her safe." James tipped his hat to Mama and Ben, then he helped me lift our valises and picnic basket onto the train.

I did not dare look back. The expression of wrenching pain in Mama's eyes almost pulled me back down the steep iron steps. However, I was resolute. I had made my stand against my mother and stepfather. I had chosen to go with James, a man my parents did not know, and who I knew only from stolen moments when I was able to sneak away from home to meet him in secret. I adored him. He was so handsome and said the sweetest things to me, and when he touched my hand or kissed me, he set my heart aflutter and made my body burn. Now, I held my head high and stifled my desire for one last look at Mama's distraught face and my fear of the future I had so rashly chosen.

Earlier that week, in the beautiful drawing room of our spacious home, the home that Ben had so lovingly designed and built himself. Mama had called me an angry, thoughtless child during our last quarrel. I didn't care. I was leaving my childhood behind in the small New Hampshire village where I grew up in my search for a new life. I felt very grown up at seventeen and knew what I wanted.

"Please think carefully before you make any hasty decisions," Mama had implored.

"We have already made up our minds."

Ben said "I forbid you to go. We do not know this man!"

"You are not my father," I spat at Ben. "There is nothing you can do. I have made up my mind." I saw him recoil as if he had been physically struck as I whirled out of the room. I had a momentary flash of guilt at hurting my parents, especially Ben–he had always been kind to me. But in that moment, it did not matter.

That was just a few days before James and I boarded the train with only a few possessions, our youthful idealism and sense of adventure to sustain us.

For more information and reviews, please visit

www.caryflanagan.com

Made in the USA
Coppell, TX
03 December 2021

66793843R10184